HALF WITTED

A SQUEAKY CLEAN IN BETWEEN MYSTERY
BOOK 1

CHRISTY BARRITT

CHAPTER 1
10:56 A.M

"GABBY, I just need you to stay here with the dead guy for thirty, forty minutes max." Toby Palestine pressed a key into my hand as we stood outside a rundown house in a sketchy area of Norfolk, Virginia.

I stared at my acquaintance, certain I hadn't heard him correctly. "What? I'm here only as a favor to you. Why are you leaving me here with a corpse?"

"My girl, Angelique, is mad at me, and I have to make things right before I lose her forever. I just need to see her face-to-face. I *know* I can convince her to forgive me." Every word he said was expressed with animated hand motions and fervent inflections.

My wiry, pale-skinned friend looked like a wreck with his wispy reddish-brown hair and oversized, shapeless clothes.

I narrowed my eyes at his flimsy explanation. "This can't wait until after the job is done?"

"No, it can't." He stared at me with soulful green eyes, silently pleading with me to understand. "This girl is all I've got. She's the night to my day. The shiver to my timbers. The rocks in my river. The—"

I held up a hand to stop him before he got carried away. "So what you're saying is . . . you really like her?"

"Exactly. If I lose her, I lose everything. Understand?"

The little con artist . . . Songs from "The Music Man" began to play in my mind as they did every time I sniffed out someone trying to manipulate me.

I gave Toby a look before accepting the key from him and sighing. "Fine. But you'd better be back within forty minutes. Not one minute late either."

He grinned and clasped my shoulder with his bony, dry-knuckled hand. "I knew if anyone could handle this job, it would be you. You're into all kinds of gross stuff."

"That sounds insulting . . . and weird." Yet his statement was kind of true. But still . . .

He gave me a look. "You know what I mean. You clean up bloody crime scenes for a living, so I figured you, of all people, could handle transporting dead bodies with me until Ricky gets back from his hospital stay."

That was nice. Just what I wanted to be known for. The girl who could handle gross stuff. Who didn't mind hanging out with dead bodies.

"Why is Ricky in the hospital again?"

"We had a contest to see who could stuff the most Nerf balls up our noses. He won—but he also won a trip to the ER. Then he had some complications and —well, you don't want to know the rest."

I resisted another sigh and nodded. Toby was right. I didn't want to know.

Before I could say anything else, Toby hurried back to his SUV—the one that the funeral home let him use for work.

There was no way I was putting a dead body in the back of my van—even if it was my work van, a vehicle where I commonly placed hazmat materials to be taken to the hospital for disposal. I was talking bodily fluids, blood, and other things the average person would rather ignore.

Toby had explained to me that most people assumed hearses came to get dead bodies to transport them to the funeral home, but they didn't. Mostly because sometimes body removal technicians had to go places that were difficult to get to and required an all-terrain vehicle.

I was learning new things every day.

As Toby squealed away in the SUV, I sighed one more time and turned to the small, neglected house behind me.

It was in a not-so-great area of town, about fifteen minutes from where I lived. News reports covered happenings in the area daily. The crime rate was so high here I was tempted to go door-to-door handing out discount flyers for my crime-scene cleaning business—buy one death-scene cleanup, get one 50 percent off.

But I didn't think local law enforcement would appreciate my entrepreneurial efforts.

Instead, I turned toward the door and shoved the key into the lock. As soon as I opened the door and stepped inside, a horrible smell hit me.

I recognized it.

It was the beginning of decomposition—and it was only going to get a lot worse from here on. Unfortunately, I was all too familiar with the odor. In my line of work, the stench was a common occurrence—and one I never got used to.

I left the front door open, but the screen door was closed over the opening. I knew if I closed the thick wood door, the smell inside would never air out. If I had known how bad it would be, I would have brought my air scrub with me.

I still wasn't sure why I'd let Toby talk me into this job. It had bad idea written all over it. I suppose I was desperate for some spending money.

I'd met Toby through my job as a crime-scene cleaner. We'd struck up a conversation when he was late in removing a murdered body out of someone's shed, and I'd arrived early to clean up the leftovers.

We ran in the same circles, so to speak—the circles of death.

With his coworker, Ricky, in the hospital, Toby had called me. Apparently, his caseload was over-whelming right now, and he needed help. He got approval from the owner of the funeral home for me to assist him today.

That was fine since I didn't have any crime scenes to clean on my docket or any job quotes to give. Since people didn't schedule being victims of crimes, I never knew when I'd get a call. My business was my top priority.

I'd told Toby that, so he knew this wasn't going to become the norm.

What I hadn't known was that he really needed a body-sitter.

I sighed and glanced around before passing through the house.

As I did, I began to sing softly.

Oh, what an abysmal morning.

Oh, what an abysmal day.

I've got an abysmal feeling.

That nothing is going my way.

I thought the song had potential.

In my free time, I liked to quote musicals and make up jingles for my crime-scene cleaning business.

I knew it was weird, but I was weird, so that was okay.

I began to wander through the house, which didn't appear as if it had been updated in years. Pea green carpet stretched beneath me. Brown and orange couches were shoved against the walls. A bookshelf full of knickknacks pressed against another wall.

I paused in the kitchen and picked up a business card on the counter near the toaster oven.

Good Tidings Home Health Care and Hospice.

Toby had told me the man who'd passed away, Earl Mansfield, had been in hospice care. That meant that when he passed, the police didn't have to be called. Instead, a doctor with the agency came by to confirm the manner of death and sign the death certificate.

Earl had been dead for approximately twenty-four hours before his body had been discovered by his nurse when she checked on him last night.

Toby and I had been tasked with moving Earl from his home to the mortician's office. I hoped he would pay me for the time I had to hang around here waiting.

I picked up a greeting card towering upright beside the Good Tidings information.

I probably shouldn't have done it—it wasn't any of my business—but I read the words inside.

Get well soon.

The words were written in a condensed, block-style handwriting, and no name had been signed.

Get well soon? Hadn't the sender realized Earl had terminal cancer? Maybe the sender was trying to be kind and cheery but had been confused.

I had no idea, but I put the card back down on the counter.

I continued pacing the small kitchen, trying to pass time until Toby got back, before pausing by the back door.

I squinted when I saw specks of dirt on the yellow and beige linoleum.

The sediments looked fresh.

It was probably nothing, but the detail seemed to beg for my attention, nonetheless.

From what Toby had told me, Earl had no family

nearby to take care of him, which was why I was here alone. Often, families were present to oversee the removal process.

In this case, Earl's friend had dropped a housekey off at the funeral home this morning on his way to work.

The dirt probably didn't mean anything. Despite that, I stored the fact away in the back of my mind.

I hesitated several minutes before finally pacing down the short hallway toward the bedroom where I knew Earl Mansfield waited for me.

I hesitated a moment before stepping into the room.

I usually saw the aftermath of the situation—the remnants of crime and death that were left behind. It was my job to scrub a room or building clean from any evidence of those things so people could forget about the tragedy and move on.

In theory.

This time, I felt ahead of the curve.

I stared at the man lying in a hospital bed in the small bedroom.

Earl had probably been in his late fifties, with dark hair and a full face. He'd worked for an HVAC company and was single.

From what Toby told me, the man had died of liver cancer.

I paused as I observed him.

Why were his arms raised in the air like that? Usually, when rigor mortis set in, gravity pulled the limbs down.

But his arms were slightly extended, almost as if he'd died on his side but had later been turned over. He'd died thirty-six hours ago, so rigor was beginning to fade as decomposition began.

Perhaps when the doctor examined him, the physician had turned Earl on his back, but the man's arms remained raised.

That explanation made sense.

Maybe.

I leaned closer to Earl's hands, something about them catching my eye.

A green substance was wedged beneath his fingernails.

I might expect dirt—maybe. But the green substance threw me.

Carpet fibers? Had the man fallen, tried to get up, and fibers had been left under his nails as a result?

If a fall had happened, would home health workers have any record of it?

I leaned closer again.

But the green substance didn't look like carpet fibers. It almost looked like . . . some other kind of fiber.

Strange.

I reminded myself not to think too much of it.

Instead, I stepped back, the odor in the room getting to me.

I've got an abysmal feeling nothing is going my way.

The lyrics still played in my head.

I needed to stop thinking like the CSI I wanted to be and simply wait for Toby to return.

But, as usual in my life, that was easier said than done.

———

Thirty minutes later, Toby still wasn't back, and he wasn't answering his phone.

I was getting annoyed.

I had other things to do—I didn't know exactly what those things were, but I knew I had to do them.

And I hated feeling like my time was being wasted.

Even more than that, I hated the smell in this house.

Though I was growing nose blind to the odor, just the thought of what my lungs were breathing in made disgust roil inside me. At least, when I cleaned crime scenes, I had the whole hazmat suit thing going on.

I wandered back into the kitchen and opened the back door, quickly observing the dirt again.

I took my cell phone and snapped a picture of it, just in case.

Just in case what, Gabby?

I wasn't sure.

I stepped out into the backyard, leaving the door open to let the cool October breeze flow through the house.

The backyard matched the inside of the house with its shades of green, brown, and yellow. The lawn was overgrown, with lots of trash littering it, but I suppose that was to be expected given the circumstances.

Despite that, I found a few stepping stones, and I pretended like I was playing Frogger as I jumped from one to another.

The neighbor behind Earl was working on putting together a shed. He glanced at me and nodded before getting back to work.

It was almost as if he didn't give a second thought to my presence.

I certainly hoped if one of my neighbors saw someone strange hopping around in my backyard that they might question it.

But I didn't know very much about this Earl guy either. Maybe he wasn't personable. Maybe he was a terrible neighbor, for that matter. Maybe he was one of those guys who called the city for every infraction—out-of-date license plates, music being played too loud, or dogs that barked too much. Or maybe he was the one with out-of-date plates and loud music.

I continued to hop from stone to stone, feeling like I was getting some exercise, at least.

As I did, the neighbor began using his drill. The sound filled the air, much louder than I'd anticipated.

I wasn't sure how much longer I'd be able to stay out here. As much as I loved the sixty-degree weather and refreshing breeze, the noise grated on my nerves.

Maybe my next plan of action would be to sit in my van and listen to some music to pass the time until Toby came back.

As I leapt from stone to stone, my thoughts raced through everything that happened in my life over the past couple of months.

They stopped on Riley.

He was my new neighbor who'd moved into the apartment across the hall from me. And he was a lawyer. Handsome. Confident. Someone with a good heart.

And also someone who'd been engaged to another woman and hadn't told me.

I frowned and leapt across two stones this time.

I really wished he had let me know that before my feelings had begun to grow like a chia pet at the hands of an overeager toddler.

But the good news was that I was dating Detective Chip Parker now. I tended to date guys who weren't good for me, and I hoped Parker didn't fall into that category. The mere fact I had to ask myself that question raised some red flags in my mind. That was why I would take things slow.

That was practically my nickname. Gabby Slow-and-Easy St. Claire. Slow and easy like homemade chili. Or Sunday mornings. Or turtles.

Finally, I sighed. I couldn't take listening to that annoyingly high-pitched drill any longer.

I tried calling Toby one more time, but he still didn't answer.

So I shoved my phone into the back pocket of my ripped jeans.

I stepped back into the house and headed toward the front door.

I paused when I got there, and my back muscles tensed.

Why did something feel different?

I couldn't pinpoint what it was. But my gut told me that something in this room had been altered from when I'd been in here last.

That's when I noticed the screen door wasn't latched.

And I had *definitely* latched it.

Tension crept up my spine.

I swallowed before walking back to check on Earl one more time.

But when I reached his room, I jerked to a stop.

His bed was . . . empty.

Earl was gone.

CHAPTER 2
11:34 A.M

I STARED at the empty bed, my thoughts racing.

Had Toby come to get Earl's body and not realized I was in the backyard?

Had the funeral home director hired someone else?

Or what if something nefarious had happened? What if . . . the body had been stolen out from under me?

I ran my hand through my hair, leaving my red curls standing on end.

No. That was ridiculous. Almost as ridiculous as the idea that Earl had come back to life and walked out of here.

Wait . . . what? That wasn't a possibility . . . was it?

I was clearly losing my mind.

I rushed back to the front door and ran into the front yard. But there was no sign anyone had been here. No sign other than the front door being unlatched.

I would have heard someone come inside and steal Earl's body, right?

Except the drill from the neighbor's house would have covered any noises.

I sighed as my frown deepened.

What was I going to do now?

Just then, I saw Toby's burgundy SUV pull to a stop in front of the house.

How would I explain this?

He rushed from the vehicle and met me on the porch. His eyes were red-rimmed and his motions frantic.

"It didn't go well, Gabby. It didn't go well at all." He ran a hand over his face. "I even tried to sing 'I Will Always Love You' by Dolly Parton to her. It didn't work."

I was super sorry about his love life, but I had bigger worries right now. "Did you take Earl?"

"Did I take Earl?" Toby seemed to snap out of his heartbreak for a moment. "What are you talking about?"

"He's gone."

"Gone?" His voice rose. "What do you mean *gone*?"

He started toward the house to see for himself, but I grabbed his arm to stop him. "He's not there."

As he let out some choice words, I reluctantly released his arm.

"What happened?" His voice rose as he turned toward me.

He was talking loud enough to draw attention— which was the last thing we needed.

I shushed him before saying, "I'm still trying to figure it all out. One minute, he was in his bed. I stepped out to the backyard to get some fresh air and, when I came back inside, he was gone."

Toby ran a hand over his face again. "You've *got* to be kidding me."

"I wish."

"You had one job, Gabby. *One job*."

I couldn't even argue with him. He was right.

How had I failed so miserably?

"Could the funeral home have sent somebody else?" I decided to throw out that theory as one last desperate lifeline.

"No! We're short-staffed. There's no one to send." Despair filled his tone.

"Then maybe . . . two funeral homes were accidentally booked, and the other one came to get him."

"Gabby! Don't be ridiculous. No one else wants his body."

"Well, clearly someone did." I hated to state the obvious, but . . .

Toby began pacing the dry, withered lawn. "What am I going to do? I can't afford to lose this job. Angelique will never take me back then."

Great. He was still worried about Angelique.

Little did I know when I was singing about my abysmal day that it really, truly would be abysmal.

"What do we do now?" I crossed my arms as I watched Toby frantically pacing as if his survival depended on the constant movement.

"We've got to find that body. We need to have it to the funeral home in three hours or I could lose this job."

I flinched as my brain registered his words—both spoken and unspoken. "Wait . . . *we*? You want *me* to help?"

"Yes! This is all your fault. Of *course* I want you to help. You *are* going to help. Because if I'm going down, you're going down with me." He paused from pacing long enough to give me an accusatory stare.

"All my fault?" I had so many arguments I could make against that statement. But I didn't make them right now.

Toby was already entirely too emotional. Besides,

maybe a small part of me was intrigued. I needed to know what had happened to Earl. My curiosity demanded it.

"Maybe we should call the police," I suggested.

"No!" His eyes widened. "That's a terrible idea. We need to do everything in our power to find him first—before we get them involved."

I knew some people were opposed to involving the police in their affairs. Everyone had their own reasons. It didn't surprise me that Toby only wanted to bring them in as a last resort.

And it wasn't as if Earl was in imminent danger—especially since he was already dead. If he had been alive, this would be a totally different story.

It was too early to panic . . . in theory.

"Where do you suggest we begin?" I recrossed my arms as I waited for his answer.

"We can start by asking the neighbors if they saw anything."

I'd solved a big case not so long ago involving a senator, *and* I was dating a detective, which almost made me feel like I could be a semiprofessional investigator. I mean, I was at least at Jessica Fletcher level.

The only problem was I'd almost gotten myself killed last time I'd solved a case, so . . .

I didn't need to think about that now.

"I think talking to the neighbors is a good place to start," I told him. "Let's see if anyone saw someone leave this house . . ."

"With a dead body?" Toby finished, blinking at me with a dumbfounded look in his eyes.

I cringed. "I'm not sure how people are going to react if we say it that way. Besides, we need to keep this hush-hush. What if we just ask if anyone saw anybody suspicious out here within the last thirty minutes?"

Toby nodded quickly. "Good idea. How about I take this side of the street and you take the other side? Let's see what we can find out."

I thought that sounded like a decent plan. But we still had to cover the question of why. *Why* would someone other than a body mover take this guy?

Then I remembered the green substance I'd seen under Earl's fingernails. The dirt by the back door.

What if someone had stolen Earl because his death hadn't been as natural as the doctor claimed?

People who were already knocking on death's door . . . their murders might be a little easier to cover up.

I kept those thoughts in the back of my mind as I headed toward the house across from Earl's.

I rang the bell, but no one answered. It was the middle of the day, so I wasn't entirely surprised.

Then I went to the next house. As soon as my feet hit the porch, it sounded as if a whole army of dogs barked at me from the inside in some kind of canine war cry.

Finally, the door opened, and a militant-looking man with deep set eyes stared at me as he held back his pack of pit bulls.

"What do you want?" he grumbled.

"Hi there." I used my most cheery voice. "I'm Gabby, and I'm working with the funeral home on Earl's final arrangements."

"Who is Earl?"

Okay . . . "Earl was your neighbor across the street who recently passed away."

His expression remained unchanged as he grunted the words, "I didn't know him."

"Well, that's okay that you didn't know him. I'm just wondering if you happened to be outside and see anything strange within the past thirty minutes?"

"I've been inside watching my soaps. I wasn't paying attention to anything outside. Don't judge me. Soaps are my guilty pleasure."

"No judgment here." I took a step back, realizing this conversation wasn't going anywhere. "Sorry to interrupt."

I headed down the steps, ready to head to the next house and hope I had better luck there.

The man called to me before I reached the sidewalk. "My dogs *were* barking a little while ago."

I paused and glanced back at him. "What?"

He scowled as if he didn't like repeating himself. "My dogs. About fifteen minutes ago. They all started barking like they saw or heard something happening outside. Just like I trained them."

This guy was definitely edgy.

"You didn't see what they were barking at?" I asked.

"Nope. But they usually reserve that bark for the mailman or anyone else they perceive as an enemy."

I glanced at the three pit bulls staring at me around this guy's legs, thankful they hadn't put me in that category.

I was ready to get out of here.

"Thank you for your help," I rushed.

Okay, so maybe I wasn't totally losing my mind. Maybe the dogs had noticed something going on outside.

But that still didn't give me a clue about who might have taken Earl's body. Or where he could be right now, for that matter.

Could Toby and I be arrested for losing a body?

I wasn't sure how these things worked. Panic was superseding my logic.

But I really hoped Toby was having more luck than I was.

———

Toby hadn't had any better luck than I had.

Hardly anyone had been home as we'd canvassed the houses nearby.

Of the few people we spoke with, no one had noticed anything. In fact, none of the neighbors had really even known Earl.

That meant Toby and I were no closer to finding the truth than we'd been earlier.

I'd even looked for any cameras on the doorbells of nearby houses.

I hadn't seen any.

I paused a moment, and I tried to think about what Riley or Parker might tell me.

Let's see . . . Riley would warn me to be careful, and Parker would tell me to stay away.

That wasn't helpful.

Toby began pacing the lawn again. "I can't believe the body is gone. I can't believe I'm going to lose another job. This is the best job I've had in a long time."

Moving dead bodies was his best job? It made me

wonder what his worst job was. But I wasn't about to ask.

"Then stay positive," I told him. "There's still a really good chance we can find Earl."

"How? Oh, Gabby . . . what am I going to do?" Toby held his head in his hands as if he were under extreme mental duress. "If I lose this job, then I'm not only going to lose my girl, but I'll lose my apartment. I might even lose my car also."

"Toby, I think you're exaggerating this. Certainly, you'll be able to find another job."

"You have no idea! I'm a *terrible* employee. The only reason I got this job was because my uncle pulled some strings."

I frowned. That didn't sound good. "I'm sure something will work out for you."

Toby suddenly straightened and drew in a deep breath. "You know what? I can bum a ride off my friends and crash at your place for a while if I have to, right?"

Now *that* sounded like a truly terrible idea. Toby liked to flick his toe jam across the room and have farting contests with his friends. I only knew that because he'd invited me to hang out once.

What a mistake.

We *definitely* needed to find Earl so Toby could keep his job.

And what about my job?

A surge of panic washed through me.

If, by some chance, I was charged over this, it could seriously hinder my efforts to become an official crime-scene investigator. They wouldn't hire someone with a record.

What could I be charged with?

I wasn't sure. But I'd seen things go down in dirty ways before. What if I took the fall?

That could even affect my crime-scene cleaning business if people thought I had a criminal record.

A new sense of urgency filled me, and I turned to Toby. "Okay, let's find out *why* he was taken. If we can figure that out, then maybe we can figure out *where* he was taken."

Toby eyed me. "You really think so?"

"I do. So this is what we're going to do. You're going to go to all the nearby businesses and see if they have any security cameras they'll let you look at. You're going to see if there are any suspicious-looking vehicles that went past at the approximate time Earl may have been taken."

I knew it was a wild goose chase, but I needed to give Toby something to do. I didn't trust him to do any of the other tasks I had in mind.

"And what are you going to do?" He eyed me as if I was setting him up.

"You said a friend of Earl's arranged for his body to be picked up, right? He's your contact?"

"That's right. Anthony Redfield. Since Earl had no family, Anthony decided to make some final arrangements for his friend. Nothing fancy or expensive, but at least Earl won't be indigent—you know, unclaimed and overseen by the government."

"I'm going to go talk to Anthony and see if there's any reason someone might want to take Earl's body. Maybe he had . . . I don't know . . . gold teeth or something."

"Are you sure it's safe to go by yourself?" Toby eyed me as if trying to guess my level of competence.

I felt much better going by myself than I did going with Toby. I nodded. "Yes, I'm sure. If we're going to find Earl in time, then we have to split up."

He nodded, almost as if relieved I hadn't asked him to come along with me.

"Okay then," he rushed. "I'll go check out the store cameras now."

I nodded and got Anthony's contact information from him. "I'll lock up the house and be right behind you."

CHAPTER 3
12:18 P.M

I WAS on the road five minutes later. I'd given Anthony Redfield a call, and he'd agreed to meet me on his lunch break from work. He was an HVAC tech with a brusque voice.

That's why I was glad we'd agreed to meet at a restaurant, somewhere public.

Just as I headed down the street, my phone rang. It was Riley.

"Hey." His voice dipped when I answered. "What's going on?"

"I'm just on my way to question someone. You?"

"Wait . . . question someone?" Surprise caught his voice. "What are you talking about?"

I explained the situation to him.

"You're meeting him at The Sunrise Diner? You'll

pass our place on the way there. Why don't you pick me up?"

"You want to go with me?" I hadn't seen that one coming.

"Yeah, I do. I'd feel better if you weren't alone, especially after what happened last time."

Last time, I'd nearly gotten myself killed when I was cleaning a crime scene and found a weapon the killer had concealed. Then I'd nearly drug my friends into my mess with me.

"Are you sure Veronica will be okay with this?" I pressed my lips into a frown as soon as the words left my mouth. I shouldn't have said that, but it was too late to take it back.

"Veronica and I are no longer together," Riley reminded me. "I think I should be asking you about Parker instead."

"He'll just be glad I didn't ask him to come along."

I thought Riley might laugh, but he didn't. Riley and Parker weren't the biggest fans of each other.

"The man can be gruff sometimes," Riley finally said.

"Yes, but he's a teddy bear inside," I said the words dryly, knowing they weren't true.

Parker really wasn't a teddy bear on the inside.

He was a prickly—but handsome—cactus, inside and out.

I ended my call and took a slight detour to pick up Riley. I still should be on time to meet Anthony, however.

A few minutes later, Riley hopped in the van with me.

As soon as I saw his lithe figure step from the apartment complex, my heart quickened. It wasn't that he was the most gorgeous man I'd ever seen. But the two of us just connected—which was weird because it was so unlikely.

Riley was upper middle class and well educated. I'd grown up poor and had to drop out of college. I now worked a blue-collar job.

I knew a future between the two of us wasn't plausible.

Which was why it was better that I was dating Parker now. Our backgrounds were similar.

But my heart didn't race the same way around Parker as it did with Riley.

"How's it going?" Riley asked as he glanced at me and pulled his seatbelt on.

I was pretty sure he'd just shaven. I could smell his minty aftershave—and I liked it a little too much.

"It's been a day," I said as I pulled away. "An abysmal day."

"Abysmal? Interesting word choice."

"Isn't it?" I resisted singing him the song I'd come up with. "Is it true I could be arrested for losing a dead body?"

He winced. "I doubt you'd be arrested for that. It wasn't as if you were desecrating a corpse or treating the remains in a disrespectful manner. I'd say your biggest worry will be the funeral home and the repercussions they might have. They could be sued over this, probably for negligence."

My stomach sank. "And then they could sue me in return?"

"I didn't say that. I mean, you didn't steal the body or do anything wrong other than being there when it was snatched. But people are litigation happy, so it's a possibility. And the fact you haven't reported the crime . . . well, that won't look good either."

I tried not to pout even though I *really* wanted to.

"You couldn't have known . . ." Riley muttered.

His words made me feel better.

But even if this wasn't a crime, a lot was still on the line—including my sanity and possibly my future.

Finally, I pulled up to the diner and put my van in Park.

Now I prayed Anthony had some of the answers we were looking for.

——————

Anthony had thick dark hair cut in a spiky style, was on the shorter side, and had uncountable tattoos stretching across his arms and up his neck.

I told the man I'd pay for his meal, and I was nearly certain he ordered the most expensive thing on the menu—steak with mashed potatoes, peppers, and onions.

I thought about my dwindling bank account and instantly regretted my offer. Then I simply ordered a lemonade, feigning that I wasn't hungry.

Riley glanced at me, and I could tell he was trying to read me and ascertain whether or not I really was hungry.

I was certain he'd pay if I let him. He was a lawyer and brought in a much better paycheck than I did as a crime-scene cleaner. But he wasn't currently working, and he was still trying to get his license to practice law in Virginia since he'd recently moved here from California.

But a girl still had some pride, you know?

I didn't wait until the food came to question Anthony.

"Thanks for meeting me." I shifted my feet beneath me, and my flip-flops stuck to the floor. That's how you really knew you were in a classy establishment—sticky floors.

They were just my speed.

"Why do you want to know about Earl?" Anthony stared at me and then Riley. "And who are you again?"

I cleared my throat. I couldn't simply go into this conversation admitting I was a temporary body mover who'd lost the corpse I'd been charged with transporting.

That wouldn't sound good, and word would probably get back to the funeral home, which would result in Toby being fired and trying to crash at my place.

That wasn't going to happen.

So I'd come up with a cover story.

"I run the investigative arm of Good Tidings Home Health Care and Hospice," I started, feeling only slightly guilty for my fib. "This is my colleague, Riley. He's a lawyer for the agency."

Anthony's eyes narrowed. "Home health care agencies have investigators?"

"Death is a big business." I nodded as if I understood how morbid my words might sound.

His eyebrows flicked before he seemed to accept that. "I guess. So what do you need?"

"I understand you're making arrangements for Earl upon his death."

A frown tugged at his lips. "That's right. Someone had to do it. I didn't just want him to be cremated and forgotten, you know? That didn't seem right."

"I understand." I took a sip of my lemonade before asking, "What was Earl like?"

Anthony stared at me another moment, his thoughts clearly churning. "What exactly are you investigating here?"

I'd thought this through also.

"We always do a final interview before closing our cases . . . our health care cases." I cringed, knowing how lame my words sounded. "You know how paperwork is. Document, document, document. I blame it on government overreach."

"Earl was a good guy," Anthony started, a forlorn look in his eyes as he dragged his gaze to meet mine. "He kept to himself mostly, but I knew him pretty well."

"He worked with you at the HVAC company?" I clarified. "Just Chill, correct?"

I'd seen their commercials on TV. They used the song "Cold as Ice" by Foreigner, and the jingle was really pretty catchy. The workers even wore sunglasses and British rock attire as they sang and danced on the screen.

"That's right. We worked together for about twelve years. Made a pretty good team if I had to say so myself."

"I can imagine. What did Earl like to do when he wasn't working for the HVAC company?"

"Gamble. Drink. Smoke. Lots of habits people would consider to be pretty unhealthy."

I nodded in agreement. "Did he ever get himself in trouble doing those things?"

The answer to that question was almost always a resounding yes.

"Maybe, but nothing too serious. I mean, really, the guy was fairly quiet, and he liked to be by himself." He shrugged and flicked a crumb from the table.

"Was Earl ever married?" Riley asked before taking a sip of his coffee.

Before Anthony could answer, our food was delivered.

Riley lifted up a quick prayer before digging into his club sandwich and fries. When he offered me a fry, I took one.

This place may have sticky floors, but their French fries were the bomb. I was going to have to snitch a few more.

"Earl was married once." Anthony used his knife to saw into his steak. "It only lasted a year, though. The two loved as hard as they fought. But the fighting won."

"How long ago was that?" I asked.

He let out a thinking sound before saying, "They probably split about a year ago."

That was recent enough for his ex to be a suspect here. "And does his ex-wife still live in this area? I'm surprised she hasn't had more to do with his final arrangements. Even though they're divorced, it's not entirely unusual for an ex to get involved—especially if there's a will."

I actually had a long conversation with a mortician about that once. Strange, but the facts were coming in handy now.

"No," Anthony said. "Daphne hated him."

Now *that* was interesting. Passion that strong could lead to desperate things.

Desperate things like stealing a body.

Taylor Swift's "I Knew You Were Trouble" began to play in my mind.

"You said her name is Daphne?" I asked before taking a sip of my bittersweet lemonade.

"That's right. Daphne Mansfield."

I stored her name in the back of my mind.

"Did Earl have any other enemies?" Riley asked before pushing his plate toward me again.

I took another fry.

"No, he was a nice, likable guy that no one had problems with." Anthony shrugged before putting an enormous bite of steak in his mouth and chomping on it.

I frowned.

Somehow, I didn't believe that no one had any problems with Earl.

Because, in my experience, everyone had enemies.

Sometimes those enemies were even disguised as friends.

CHAPTER 4
1:26 P.M

BACK IN MY VAN, I let out a sigh.

Riley had somehow gotten to the waitress before me and paid the bill. I wanted to complain, but I couldn't.

The thirty-two-dollar bill could have made the difference between groceries or no groceries for me. This was simply the reality of my life right now.

When I had the money, I'd figure out a way to pay Riley back.

As we sat in my van, I didn't bother to move.

I could just tell the police about this. However, what if I was charged with negligence? That could ruin my chances of ever being hired by the police department. My dreams of becoming an official CSI would be over.

I had to fix this.

Riley leaned back in his seat. "Why would someone steal a body?"

"That's the question I'm trying to figure out." I sighed again and crossed my arms.

"Maybe his death wasn't natural," Riley offered. "Maybe the doctor made a mistake."

"I thought about that also. But if that's the case, then whoever killed him was on the road to getting away with this. Why steal the body and possibly draw attention to it?"

Riley shrugged. "Maybe this thief wanted something Earl had."

"Something he had? It's not like his organs could be harvested. He was way too dead for that." I straightened. "Maybe this person needed a dead body so they could drive in the carpool lane."

Riley gave me a look. "Gabby . . ."

"What?" I raised my voice in fake outrage. "That's just as crazy as the other ideas we've come up with!"

"You'll figure it out," Riley's voice sounded reassuring. "Just don't get yourself into any trouble in the meantime. If you need anything, you know you can call me."

I thanked him and then started my van. A few minutes later, I dropped Riley off at our apartment complex.

Just as I did, Toby called.

Some of the glumness was gone from his voice. *That* had me interested.

"What's going on?" I asked as I gripped the wheel.

"I think I found the car used to steal Earl."

Now *that* was a twist that I hadn't seen coming. I'd had zero hope Toby would be successful—for more than one reason. But the top reason was because he seemed wholly incompetent.

Then again, I was the one who'd had the body stolen on my watch, so I didn't have much room to talk.

"How can you be sure it's the right car?" Questions raced through my mind.

"Because there was a foot hanging out the back window."

———

I headed back to Earl's house.

When I arrived, I spotted Toby sitting on the porch with hunched shoulders and a downcast expression. He quickly set his water bottle down beside him when he saw me. The container was one of those refillable flasks, but I had to wonder what was inside.

I hoped it was water, but as I got closer, I made a mental note to check for alcohol on his breath.

I sat beside him and mirrored his body language by placing my elbows on my knees and leaning forward. I waited a moment before asking, "So?"

Toby handed me his phone.

I hit Play and noticed he'd taken a video of a video. Unfortunately, his hands weren't steady, which made it hard to tell what was really going on.

"I tried." He shrugged as if he knew what I was thinking. "It was the best I could do."

I watched as several vehicles passed on the screen. A couple of cars. An animal control vehicle. A small truck.

Finally, I paused the video when I saw an old silver sedan enter the screen. But no matter how many times I watched and replayed it, I couldn't see the license plate.

But I did see that foot.

Sure, anyone could lie in the back seat of a car with his or her foot sticking out, I supposed.

But there was something about this foot and the way it was positioned that didn't look quite natural . . . it appeared stiff, as if in the thrusts of rigor mortis.

If I had to, I could ask Parker to help me with this. He could officially track down the security footage and maybe trace a potential license plate.

But I'd only do that as a last resort. I didn't want to hear Parker's lecture when he found out I'd taken this job—and lost the dead body. The payoff wasn't worth the pain.

"What now?" Toby turned toward me. "We know the body was stolen by someone in a silver sedan. But how do we find it?"

That was an excellent question.

I clearly needed to think of something else to keep Toby occupied. Otherwise, he'd only hinder any progress I might make.

Before I could suggest anything, it turned out Toby had a better idea.

"Robert—my boss—called and asked where I was."

I held my breath. "And you said?"

"I told him there had been a little hang-up here with Earl's friend, and I was waiting for the guy to say his final goodbye."

"Fast thinking. And?"

"Robert asked if I could go do another job in the meantime. But that means both of us will need to go. I can't load the body on my own."

Um . . . that wasn't going to work. "But if I'm with you, then I can't look for Earl."

"I know. What am I supposed to do?" Toby threw

his hands in the air, his emotions clearly getting the best of him.

This seriously wasn't my problem. "Don't you have anyone else you could call to help you?"

He thought about it a moment before shrugging. "Maybe I could call Steve. He owes me one."

"Is he trustworthy?" I'd had to get a background check before being able to do this job. Apparently, there were sick people out there! Why else would a background check be necessary?

"Yeah, man. He's trustworthy. He let me hang out at his place that one time when the police were chasing me. Even lied for me."

"The police chased you?"

"I got into a fight with someone at this restaurant—"

"Not a bar?" I interrupted.

"Naw, it was a restaurant. Well, more of a bakery. Some guy ordered the last chocolate cupcake right in front of my face!"

I pressed my eyes closed. "So you got into a fist fight?"

"He wouldn't give it up. Anyway, my bro Steve is solid."

I resisted an eyeroll.

"Okay, why don't you talk to Steve?" I finally

said. "That will buy us some time. In the meantime, I'll keep looking for Earl."

Toby paused and scratched his head. "How are you going to find him?"

"I'm going to talk to his ex-wife and then some of the staff at the home health agency."

"Do you think any of those people will have any answers?"

I shrugged. "I can't say for sure. But it's a good place to start."

CHAPTER 5

1:55 P.M

JUST AS I'D told Toby, I would start with the ex-wife and then question someone affiliated with the home health care agency.

It wasn't hard for me to do a quick online search and find a profile for Daphne Mansfield that included her address.

That wasn't very wise of her, but it wasn't my job to explain internet safety to anyone. Instead, I headed to her place, which was only about ten minutes away.

It was an older apartment complex surrounded by probably ten other buildings that looked exactly the same. Many of them had window AC units installed, and a lot of trash was scattered outside the buildings, overflowing from trashcans, and causing a stench in the air.

I checked Daphne's address again just to be sure I was in the right place before heading up a flimsy metal staircase to a second-story apartment. I tried the doorbell but didn't hear any noises on the other side. So I knocked instead.

Then I waited.

When there was no answer, I tried again.

"She ain't home," a scratchy voice said behind me.

I swirled around and saw a seventy-something woman standing there holding two plastic grocery bags in her thin, wrinkled arms. I hadn't even heard her come up the stairs.

I had to be sharper than this. What if she'd been an assassin? I'd be dead right now!

"She's not?"

The woman shook her head, not hiding her suspicion of me as she headed to the door across the breezeway. "She works until three every day."

"You don't, by chance, have a phone number where I could call her, do you?"

"Nope." The woman jammed her key into the lock.

I knew I was running out of time. "Any chance you know where she works?"

"Don't know the name of it, but she travels a lot. I

try not to ask her too many questions because she talks entirely too much. I got other things to do."

"She travels?" I was trying to put together a mental image of Daphne.

"That's right. I don't think she has an office. She just goes from place to place trying to sell solar panels. Even tried to sell me some even though she knows good and well I live in an apartment complex!"

Wow, that took some nerve. I'd gotten caught by one of those salespeople before also, and the conversation had been painful.

"I'm pretty sure she's on the road right now making her rounds—she left early this morning. But, like I said, she's usually back home by three."

With that said, the elderly woman opened her door and slipped inside.

I guessed that was it.

It looked like I'd need to skip to the next thing on my list for now.

Good Tidings Home Health Care and Hospice.

———

My mind raced on my way to Good Tidings.

I couldn't simply barge in and explain that we'd

lost this guy's body and expect someone to give me —someone with no credentials—answers.

That wouldn't get me very far.

Lying wasn't my favorite thing to do. But sometimes it seemed like a necessary evil in order to get the job done.

I'd just started to think more about God and how I felt about Him. I didn't know much, but I was nearly certain He wouldn't approve of this.

Yet, on the other hand, I was trying to find justice for someone—even if that someone was now dead. So God would smile on that, right?

I wasn't sure. I still had a lot of questions and not very many answers when it came to God.

Maybe I'd ask Riley later. He was a church boy through and through. He also had an inner peace that I didn't—but I wanted it.

For now, I opened the back of my van and pulled on a blazer.

Yes, a blazer. I may or may not keep things in the back of my van for occasions such as this.

I pulled my messy, curly red hair back into a neat bun. Then I slipped the blazer over my snarky "So Apparently, I'm Difficult" T-shirt and buttoned it, successfully concealing the words. Finally, I slipped out of my flip-flops and shoved my feet into some flats.

In an instant, I'd been transformed into a lawyer . . . or at least into someone who could pass as lawyer-ish.

That's right. I was now Gabby St. Claire, Esquire. I hoped I'd hung around Riley enough for some of his lawyer talk to rub off on me. That said, let me call your attention to exhibit number one: Gabby St. Claire Attempting to Become the Master of Disguise.

As I remembered Toby's plan to live with me if he lost his job, I decided to push forward.

I sucked in a breath and rolled my shoulders back before walking inside. I told the receptionist I needed to speak to Earl Mansfield's nurse.

The twentysomething eyed me. "Can I ask what this is pertaining to?"

"I need to find out who visited Mr. Mansfield in his final days. One of the stipulations of his will is that the people who visited will get part of his inheritance. However, I've been having trouble tracking down exactly who those people are. It's unclear right now with the way the will is written whether or not that's going to include the hospice workers. If they're nice enough, then it might."

The woman's eyes lit as if she were suddenly interested. "Let me see what I can do. What's your name again?"

"Gabby St. Claire . . . esquire." I couldn't help but add that last part.

"One moment."

I couldn't believe she'd bought my story. Did people really do that? Leave part of their inheritance based on silly stipulations?

I didn't know. It happened in movies. There were trivial conditions, like the person had to get married before they would receive any money. Or they had to perform random acts of kindness until a change of heart occurred and they became honorable, selfless citizens.

Either way, I was thankful this woman seemed to buy my flimsy explanation.

The front desk clerk obviously had no idea who this Earl guy was because I couldn't imagine he had much of an inheritance left to leave.

But sometimes people surprised me. I shouldn't be so quick to draw conclusions like that.

Several minutes later, a woman in her fifties with short, dark hair and a plump face came out and greeted me with a smile. "Ms. St. Claire? I'm Sheila. I was Mr. Mansfield's nurse."

I extended my hand, trying to look professional. But as she extended her hand back to me for a shake, the whole interaction felt stiff and awkward, and I quickly pulled away.

Good going, Gabby. Note to self: practice shaking hands more so you seem more professional.

I rubbed my hand on the side of my jeans and offered a bright smile, hoping to pass off my nerves. "Could I have a moment with you?"

"Sarah told me what was going on. Of course."

She led me back to a staff kitchenette and shut the door. A small table waited in the corner with three flimsy metal chairs around it.

"Please, have a seat," Nurse Sheila said. "Can I get you some coffee? It's from the Keurig, but it's pretty tasty. I especially like the vanilla coconut flavor."

"I'm fine. Thank you. Unfortunately, I don't have a lot of time."

I started to sweat at the thought of that.

I really hoped Toby was exaggerating when he said I could get in trouble for this. But I knew if there was a body missing that someone would need to take the blame.

Toby would probably be the first person in line for trouble. But there were no guarantees that I wouldn't get some blame.

I went through the whole spiel again about Earl, and Nurse Sheila didn't even seem to blink at my outlandish explanation for being here.

"Well, isn't that intriguing," she said instead. "Earl was always such an interesting guy."

"How long did you take care of him?" I crossed my ankles, reminding myself to be demure.

"About a month. That's when Mr. Mansfield obtained our services."

"And how often did you go to his house?"

"We went every day to check on him, take his vitals, make sure he was taking his medicine, and to make sure he didn't need anything. He was always such a charmer."

A charmer? Somehow, I couldn't picture it.

"Were you the only nurse who cared for him?" I asked.

"I was the nurse assigned to him. But another nurse, on occasion, would visit if I couldn't be there. Her name is Tamara, but she's on vacation this week. Her cousin is getting married in Montana."

"I see." I shifted in my seat and pulled out a pad of paper and pen from my purse.

I tried to keep the bag beneath the table because it didn't look very lawyer-like. It was a cognac-colored Kate Spade knockoff—but the fake leather was peeling.

My friend, Sierra, an animal rights activist, would never approve of me buying a real leather purse—even if I could afford it.

I gripped my pen in hand as I looked up at Sheila again and drew in a breath.

I hoped all of this wasn't for nothing and that this meeting would provide some answers.

CHAPTER 6
2:20 P.M

"WELL, Mr. Mansfield's ex-wife came a few days before his death," Nurse Sheila started. "It didn't go well."

"Why not?" Excitement rushed through me. Maybe I'd finally get some of the answers I was searching for. I had a feeling Nurse Sheila had a great memory.

"One of them brought up an argument they'd had several years ago about plasticware. They both kept insisting they were right and the other was wrong. It was ridiculous, and it went on and on."

"Plasticware?"

"About whether it was a waste of money or not. His ex-wife insisted the water and electricity saved by not washing as many dishes offset the cost." She shrugged. "It seemed a strange thing to argue about."

"Agreed."

"Then his friend—I think his name was Anthony—came by. The two of them seemed to be having a decent talk. They laughed a lot . . . until they didn't."

I sat up straighter. "What do you mean?"

"They had some kind of heated discussion. I couldn't hear what it was about. Then there was that other guy who came once." Sheila tapped her chin. "He didn't stay very long, though."

"Did you catch his name?"

Sheila thought about it another moment before shaking her head. "I can't say I did. But he was a big, tall guy, and his head was shaved. He didn't really talk. He kind of grunted."

"Is there anything else you can remember about him?" That was too vague for me to go on.

She thought about it another moment before slowly nodding.

"Now that you're asking, he was wearing a blue polo shirt. I'm trying to remember what the logo was." She rolled her eyes up in thought. "Oh, I know." She looked at me and grinned. "He was with the CIA."

My breath caught. "The CIA?"

Since when did they wear blue polo shirts advertising the company?

"Not that CIA. It's an animal shelter—Caring and Investing in Animals. I'm sure you've heard of it."

Realization rolled over me. That was right. Apparently, they not only took in animals people no longer wanted, but they also rehabilitated wildlife and even helped with wild animal removal in private homes. It was a one stop shop for animal heroes near and far.

"I have heard of it." I nodded, trying not to look excited. "When did this friend visit?"

"Only a couple of days ago."

"And how did Earl seem when he left?"

She shrugged. "He looked a little upset. But he brushed it off when I asked him if he was okay."

Interesting.

CIA?

I knew just the person I could talk to who could help me infiltrate this elusive organization—uh, animal shelter.

But I had two more question first. "Did you ever use the back door?"

She narrowed her eyes with confusion. "No, why would we?"

"Just curious. And this might seem off the wall,

but . . . I noticed Mr. Mansfield had some green stuff beneath his nails. Any idea what that might have been?"

Sheila thought about it a moment before shaking her head. "I have no idea."

———

Ten minutes later, I picked up my best friend, Sierra Nakamura.

My friend was a very passionate animal rights activist. Her whole life revolved around saving four-legged creatures, the fish of the sea, and birds of the air—and anything in between, excluding humans.

She was the type who would tie herself to a cow to ensure that the animal didn't get butchered. She boycotted and protested outside circuses. She wore "Meat Is Murder" T-shirts.

Whenever there was a case involving animals, I knew I could count on Sierra to offer me some help.

She climbed into my car. At least, this time she was dressed like a normal person and not like a cat as she had been one of the last times I'd picked her up. She'd staged a protest of some sort, and the more drama, the better.

"So what's going on?" She glanced at me as she clicked her seatbelt in place.

"I'm looking for a potential suspect for a case I'm working."

Sierra shifted toward me. "You're working a case?"

"Well, it's not a *case* case. I mean, it's nothing official. Actually, it's really not a case; it's a mistake. I was in charge of keeping an eye on a dead man, and he disappeared."

She flinched before doing a double take at me as if she hadn't heard correctly. "What?"

"It's a long story. Just trust me on that. But anyway, as I've been searching for him, it's led me to someone who works with an animal shelter. Apparently, he's a big burly guy who grunts a lot."

"Okay . . . and how can I help with this?"

"I know you have a relationship with the director of CIA because you like to monitor what they're doing. I'm hoping you can use one of your contacts to get us in."

She nodded slowly as she seemed to realize what I was asking. "I don't know if you know what you're asking. Megan—the director—and I didn't exactly hit it off. When she sees me, she's not going to open her arms and welcome me. In fact, she's probably going to try to think of ways to tar and feather me."

"But you both love animals. How can you be mortal enemies like that?"

"She had the nerve to call me extreme once. Can you believe that?" Sierra narrowed her eyes.

"You? Extreme? Wow. I can't believe she said that." My words weren't entirely sincere, but Sierra didn't notice.

"I know. For real. We exchanged words after that, and I haven't seen her since. I don't need anyone telling me how to do my job. Being nice doesn't always cut it when you're trying to evoke change."

I knew better than to argue—especially when Sierra used that voice.

Sierra and I pulled up to the animal shelter. I glanced at my watch.

I was officially past the three-hour window of getting Earl to the funeral home, but Toby had indicated he'd bought some time. I hoped he was right.

I sucked in a breath and decided to keep my blazer on and my hair in a bun. Maybe people would take me more seriously this way.

Then Sierra and I climbed from my van.

Here went nothing.

We'd no sooner taken three steps toward the building when a whole flock of chickens came clucking toward us from an open gate behind the building.

I glanced at Sierra. "Who let the chicks out?"

Okay, maybe I sang the words.

And maybe I added a *cluck, cluck, cluck, cluck* in place of the *woof, woof, woof, woof*.

CHAPTER 7
2:46 P.M

I RAN after the chickens and caught one.

Sierra caught another.

Then I grabbed a runaway before it ran under my van, and I stuffed it under my other arm.

The bird pecked my bicep!

"Careful! That's a rooster!" a twentysomething man called as he chased after the rest of the birds.

Sierra began running toward them and chased the other chickens back into a coop behind the building. Once all the birds were accounted for, the man shut the gate and let out a sigh.

"Thank you so much!" The man—a skinny guy in coveralls—gazed at us like we were heroes. "We owe you guys big time."

This was the opening I was looking for! I *loved* it when people said that.

Someone I'd guess was in management based on her professional attire and the Bluetooth headset in her ears, hurried to us. Her nametag read "Megan," and she was probably in her early forties, with dark hair and a round face.

Megan . . . Sierra's contact here.

And possibly her mortal enemy.

This should be interesting.

"I just heard what happened. Thank you all so much for helping." Megan's gaze stopped on Sierra, and she gasped. "*You*. What are you doing here? Trying to organize another protest? I promise, we shed blood and tears—and we bleed money—trying to do what's best for the animals under our care, and if you think—"

I had to stop her before we got totally offtrack here. "Just so you understand, we're not here to protest. Or disrupt. Or preach. Or try to ruin you in any way."

Megan stared at me. "And who are you?"

I swallowed hard. "I'm her lawyer, of course."

"Her lawyer?" Distress stretched through Megan's voice.

"It's not like that," I explained. "I'm a *good* lawyer. A nice one."

"Usually nice lawyers suck." She gave me a pointed look.

I couldn't argue with that. People wanted to hire lawyers who were sharks, didn't they?

But Riley was a nice lawyer . . . wasn't he? I mean, I'd never seen him in court or anything.

That was something I'd need to think about later. There was still a lot about Riley Thomas I needed to figure out. I had to believe, however, that integrity and justice could go hand in hand.

"So if you're not here to talk to me about a protest or threaten me, then why are you here?" Megan's gaze flickered back and forth between me and Sierra.

Sierra started to speak again, but I had a feeling she wasn't going to say anything nice. So I stepped in.

"I want to adopt a cat," I announced.

I didn't *actually* want to adopt a cat. Whenever I wanted to be around cats, all I had to do was go down to Sierra's apartment. She had five.

"A cat." Megan clasped her hands together, her eyes suddenly beaming. "Isn't that wonderful?"

I glanced at Sierra and nodded, probably too enthusiastically. "Yes, it is."

Sierra scowled and pushed her glasses up higher on her nose.

My friend was definitely in favor of starting a war. Just being here had ignited some type of animal rights passion in her tiny animal-loving body.

But I had to keep her focused—at least until I found out if this guy worked here.

Megan escorted us inside.

As she did, I noticed the pictures lining the walls beside me.

Pictures of employees.

Bingo!

I slowed my steps as I observed them. I wouldn't be able to tell the height of any of these men on this wall. So that would make it tricky. And just because the guy was bald when he went to Earl's house, didn't mean he was naturally bald. He could have hair in this picture.

The woman talked on and on about all the different cats they'd gotten in just a few days ago from a crazy hoarding situation.

Honestly, listening to her made me think I *did* need to adopt a cat.

But I wouldn't. I knew that.

I paused as one picture came into view.

Gus Stevens.

It had to be him. He fit the description of the man I was looking for.

I paused to stare at his picture, and it was only then that Megan noticed I had stopped.

"Is everything okay?" she asked.

"I feel like I know this guy." I pointed out his picture.

She paced closer to me and grinned. "Oh, yes, that's Gus. He oversees operations."

"I'm pretty sure we went to high school together."

She looked at me and blinked. "High school? That's surprising because you look so much younger. Gus is in his late forties."

I touched my bun. "So am I. I just age well."

Megan's eyes widened as if she were impressed. "I'd say you do. You must tell me your secrets."

"Well, I use . . ." My mind raced through the possibilities . . . "Chicken poop, actually."

"What?"

Sierra gave me a wide-eyed glance.

"I collect chicken poop and smear it on my face once a week. It's an old Asian ritual that Sierra taught me."

"And that's it?"

"Then I hang upside down so the blood will go to my head. I stay like that for fifteen minutes and then rinse. I swear by it."

Sierra's eyes widened even more as I went on and on about my fake beauty routine.

As soon as Megan looked away, I shrugged. I had no earthly idea what I was saying.

"Is there any chance Gus is here right now?" I asked.

"As a matter of fact, I do believe he's in his office," Megan said. "Would you like me to see?"

"If you wouldn't mind, that would be great."

We walked away from the kennel area and into an administrative hallway.

Anticipation bubbled inside me.

I hoped that Gus might have some answers for me.

———

Gus looked me up and down. "You went to Booker T? Class of 1991?"

"That's right. You don't remember me?"

He tilted his head skeptically. "I think I'd remember you."

I glanced at Sierra, giving her a silent look that begged her to distract Megan.

She cleared her throat and glanced at Megan, an annoyed look in her eyes. "I was hoping I could talk to you about an award my company is giving out to the best animal shelters in the area . . ."

"The best?" Megan raised her eyebrows. "Well, of course."

As the two moseyed away, I turned back to Gus.

"So . . . what brings you by here?" he asked, his voice lacking enthusiasm.

"I'm looking for a cat." More like a goat. A scapegoat.

"And you happened to see my picture, which led you into my office because . . ." He tilted his head in confusion. ". . . we went to high school together?"

I glanced behind me and noted that Megan was still busy talking to Sierra. Then I shut the door. "Actually, that's not true."

"Really?" Heavy sarcasm doused his words.

"The truth is I'm trying to find out some information about Earl Mansfield. I heard that you were friends."

He leaned back, his shoulders visibly tensing. "Who are you? A cop?"

"I'm more of a private investigator."

"*More* of a private investigator or an *actual* private investigator?" He raised his eyebrows, still calm, cool, and collected.

"It's just a minor detail. And I don't have much time." I stepped closer. "Is it true that you went to go see Earl during his final days?"

"I did. The two of us actually *did* go to high school together." He gave me a pointed look.

I shrugged apologetically. "I see. Were you close?"

"We used to be best friends—or BFFs as all the youngsters say nowadays."

If that was true, then this guy could be a great contact for this investigation. I needed to milk everything out of this conversation that I could.

"Did something happen between the two of you when you were visiting?" I asked. "I heard there was some tension between Earl and one of his close friends."

"Tension? Who told you that?" Gus bristled.

"That's not important."

His gaze darkened. "It must've been that nurse. She was so cheerful, but I could tell she was nosy too."

Sierra's and Megan's voices became louder in the hallway, and I knew I needed to hurry.

"Why was there tension?" I rushed.

I wasn't sure the blunt question would get me very far. It wasn't like this guy would admit that he and Earl had a falling out, and he had ultimately killed Earl, stolen his body, and put it in the back of a silver sedan.

He let out a resigned sigh. "The truth is that back in high school, Earl and I put together a bucket list. I thought that Earl and I should still try to cross some things off that list before, you know . . . he kicked the bucket."

"What was on the list?"

"We wanted to ride fifty different roller coasters. Go to a bike rave. Enter a hot dog eating contest. I said we should run a marathon. Earl wasn't in favor."

"I can understand that, although I do enjoy a good run sometimes. Still, a marathon . . . that's a lot of miles."

"The truth is I wanted him to go bungee jumping with me, and he said no. I felt like he was giving up, and I tried to convince him to change his mind. But he wouldn't."

The voices were now right outside the door. My time was up.

"And that was all?" I whispered.

"That was all. He got agitated with me. Told me I didn't understand what it was like to face death. I knew at that point there was no changing his mind, so I left. End of story."

End of story indeed.

I repressed a sigh.

This whole charade had gotten me nowhere.

And I was running out of time.

CHAPTER 8
2:54 P.M

AS SIERRA and I headed toward the exit, Megan called behind us. "What about that cat?"

"I'll have to come back later!" I yelled over my shoulder.

"I look forward to hearing about that award!"

"I'll be in touch," Sierra said with a wave.

As we climbed into my van, I gave Sierra an update on what I'd learned—which wasn't much.

"That lady is infuriating!" Sierra said, almost as if she hadn't heard me. "For one thing, they're animal companions *not* pets. Why can't people understand that?"

I listened to Sierra go on and on for several more minutes before I had to cut her off.

I was on a deadline here, and I couldn't listen to her diatribe all day.

"I'm sorry, but I need to check in with Toby," I told her.

I grabbed my phone and called Toby.

"Gabby . . . I'm glad you called," he rushed, a new excitement in his voice. "I'm on my way to pick up another body."

I leaned back in my seat. "It sounds like you're buying more time."

"That's right. My boss knows I can't get Earl right now because I have other jobs. I think he believed me when I told him Earl's friend came in to pay his final respects."

"That's good news."

"Even better, my friend Steve happened to have a curly red wig in his backpack. He wore it and stayed in the SUV, so my boss doesn't even know that you weren't with me."

"He just happened to have a red wig with him?"

"Long story."

I shook my head. Truthfully, I didn't want to know.

"Anyway, we just have to bring Earl here by the end of the day," Toby continued.

"And what time is that?"

"Six. Can you do it?"

I glanced at my watch. "We don't have much choice."

———

I dropped Sierra off back at her work and then sat in my van for a moment.

My time was running out. What should I do now?

I definitely didn't want to find Toby and listen to him rant anymore about how I'd had a corpse stolen out from under me.

I glanced at the time.

Daphne could be home by now.

Since I didn't know what else to do, I decided that maybe I should pay her another visit. Maybe I'd have more luck this time.

I pulled up to the same apartment complex and walked up the same stairs toward her same apartment.

As I passed her neighbor's place, I saw the curtain flutter. The woman must know everything that happened around here the way she kept an eye on things.

Before I could knock on Daphne's door, it opened.

A woman in her forties with big, light-brown hair gasped and jumped back from the door, her hand covering her heart as she stared at me. She was dressed in a cheap business suit—I recognized it because that's what I owned also—and her makeup was a little too heavy.

"You scared me." Daphne stared at me as if sizing me up.

"I'm sorry." I pointed to my other hand, which was poised in a fist and still in the air. "You opened the door before I could knock."

She let out a nervous laugh. "I see. Can I help you?"

"My name is Gabby, and I was hoping to ask you a few questions."

"Questions about what? I'm not really in the mood for a sale's pitch right now. I know what it's like because I do sales for a living too, but—"

"I'm not trying to sell anything. It's about Earl."

As soon as I said his name, music began playing from the woman's pocket.

I squinted.

Wait . . . was that the Dixie Chicks? And was that the song "Earl's Gotta Die"?

Her cheeks flushed as if she were embarrassed, and she quickly hit a button until the ringing stopped. "I know how that looks. Insensitive. But when I programed that song on my phone, Earl was still alive and I was really mad at him. I keep meaning to change it, but there's something nostalgic when I listen to it. It used to be our song."

I didn't even have the energy to dive into the psychology of that.

Instead, I asked, "Can you spare five minutes?"

She stared at me again and crossed her arms. "How did you know Earl?"

"I'm helping with his final arrangements. I can explain, and I promise it will make sense."

After she gave me a skeptical look, she opened her door. "Five minutes. Then I've got to run and get the takeout I ordered."

Relief washed through me.

I hoped I could get this done in five minutes.

We stepped inside her apartment, but Daphne didn't bother to offer me a seat or a drink, which was fine.

"Now, who are you?" She stared at me, still appearing skeptical as we stood in the middle of her living room.

"I work with the Norfolk police." I had so many cover stories going that I was bound to get them mixed up any time now. I should have just picked one and stuck with it.

Her eyes widened. "You didn't tell me you were with the police."

"That's because I'm not. But I work with them on occasion as a consultant." That wasn't totally the truth, but I *had* helped them solve a case so . . .

"What's this have to do with Earl? He had liver cancer." Her eyes narrowed as she stared at me.

"We're just trying to wrap up all the final details of his death. I was wondering if you noticed anything suspicious about him in his final days?"

"Suspicious?" Her voice tightened as if my question left her on edge.

"You know, out of the ordinary? The hospice nurse said you visited him a couple of days before he died."

"I didn't want the man to suffer alone. I thought it was the least I could do."

"Understandable. And he was your ex, so I'm sure it was a strained relationship. My understanding is that you weren't married long?"

"We weren't. We probably jumped into things too quickly. When you get to my age, the pickings are slim. He seemed like one of the better ones, but he wasn't. My bad luck streak continues."

I could understand what that was like. I was a good fifteen or more years younger than she was, but I'd picked some real jerks to date.

I turned my focus back to Earl, however. "So he was a bad guy?"

Daphne let out a breath. "I don't know if I'd say Earl was a bad guy. But he wasn't relationship material. He only thought of himself. I didn't get married just so I could cook and clean for someone and meet their every need. I have needs too!"

"I understand," I said. "Is there anything else you can tell me about the last couple months of his life? Did anything change other than his cancer diagnosis?"

She let out a sigh. "I don't know. I tried not to talk to him unless I absolutely had to."

Daphne stared off in the distance as if trying to search her thoughts. Finally, she glanced back at me.

"There is one thing," she murmured. "But I don't even know if it's worth mentioning."

"You can tell me, and I can be the judge of that."

I waited with anticipation for whatever she had to say.

"LAST TIME I talked to Earl, he was rambling on and on about something. He said he may have found the fountain of youth."

I stared at Daphne. That hadn't been what I expected to hear. "What?"

Her eyebrows jerked up, and her lips pulled outward in what almost looked like a temporary face lift. "Weird, right? I thought maybe some of his meds were making him loopy or something."

I shifted on the purple living room rug. "What else did he say about this fountain of youth?"

"Not much. He kept talking on and on about it as if it was supposed to make sense to me." She rolled her eyes. "I don't think it was like a physical fountain of youth. But maybe he'd discovered something he thought would help him prolong his life. I'm not sure. After a while, I just tuned him out. It was all nonsense."

"I see."

"I wish there was more I could say to help you." She glanced at her smart watch. "But I'm afraid that's all I've got, and my pu pu platter will be cold very soon."

Daphne ushered me from her apartment.

But she had given me something to think about.

———

As I walked back to my car, I heard someone call my name.

I knew without looking exactly who it was.

I froze a moment and drew in a deep breath before slowly turning and plastering on a smile. "Parker!"

My boyfriend strode across the broken sidewalk and stopped in front of me. His eyes narrowed, and he didn't exactly offer a warm kiss and greeting.

Instead, he blurted, "What are you doing here?"

"It's great to see you too." I raised my face as if anticipating a kiss.

I wasn't.

"No, really, what are you doing here? I told you

that you shouldn't come to this part of town on your own. It's dangerous for someone like you."

"And when you say someone like me, you mean . . ." I let my voice trail so Parker could finish that statement.

He scowled. "Let's just say you stand out. You may have grown up in the hood, but this is a different kind of hood. I'm just glad you didn't come here at dark."

"What are you doing here?"

"I'm investigating a shooting, of course. It's why I usually come to this area." He nodded to one of the buildings in the distance.

I spotted the crime-scene tape there. "I see."

He waited and even had the audacity to tap his foot as if I owed him an explanation.

I didn't owe him a reason. In fact, I didn't owe him anything. But maybe I was making more of a big deal over this than I should.

"I was talking to someone about something." I realized I couldn't exactly tell Parker what I was doing or he might ask more questions and then find out I'd lost a dead body.

Then he might have to arrest me. Or he might not. I still wasn't sure what the rules were about losing dead people.

"Do you have a friend who lives over here?" The

skepticism in his voice made it clear he didn't believe that explanation.

"Not really. I was just talking to a friend of a friend." That was if I wanted to consider Earl a friend.

Keeping secrets was so hard, and I was so bad at it.

He shifted and crossed his arms again. "Gabby . . ."

Warning marred his voice.

I frowned.

Should I tell him?

I wasn't sure.

But I was going to have to say something.

CHAPTER 10
3:29 P.M

I FINALLY LET out a sigh and told Parker everything.

I prayed I didn't regret it.

"You lost a dead body?" He stared at me as if I had rocks for brains.

"I stepped out the back door and, when I came back inside, this guy was gone. It's not like I misplaced him like someone misplaces their keys. He's way too big to fit in between the couch cushions."

His eyes narrowed even more. "You should have kept the front door locked."

"Why in the world would I ever think that someone would want to steal a dead body?" My voice rose as frustration welled in me. "The smell alone would be very off-putting. Not to mention the guy wasn't a lightweight."

Parker shook his head. "You really know how to get yourself into some messes."

I repressed a sigh and bit my tongue.

"You've got to figure out the motive," Parker finally offered.

I nodded, suddenly feeling excited. "I know! That's what I said too."

"What I can't think of here are many reasons why somebody would want a dead body. Could he be a drug mule?"

"A drug mule?" I repeated. I hadn't even considered that. Probably because it didn't make much sense. "In order to be a drug mule, Earl would've had to be traveling to or from another country, right?"

"Most likely."

"This guy had liver cancer, and he'd been receiving hospice care. He definitely hasn't been out of the country recently. I can't see why anyone would be a drug mule if they weren't leaving our borders."

"True." Parker's shoulders flicked up nonchalantly. "Maybe someone killed him for his life insurance."

Life insurance? Why hadn't I thought about that? That would make Daphne the most likely suspect.

But . . . "Even if he had life insurance, how would stealing the body help any of that? I could see the being murdered part of it, but . . ."

"I'm intrigued. But it sounds like you need to find a dead body *and* you have no leads."

Yes, Captain Obvious.

I kept my expression even, however. Being cordial was a good play sometimes—like now.

"You're correct: I don't have any leads," I conceded. "Well, I did hear his body was taken away in a silver sedan. Apparently, he didn't fit in the backseat very well, and his foot was hanging out one of the windows. With rigor mortis, the body thief probably wasn't able to bend Earl's legs."

"You tried the security camera footage from surrounding houses?" he asked as if my last statement hadn't even fazed him.

"Of course. Do you think I'm an amateur?" My voice held mock offense.

"And you've talked to this guy's friends? Because whoever did this obviously knew Earl. They knew he was dead, and they knew he was still in the house." He twisted his neck and gave me a corner-of-the-eye stare.

"I've talked to his friends, and I still don't know anything."

He nudged my shoulder with his fist. "Then it

sounds like you have some work to do, Gabby. I don't know what to tell you. But if you don't find him by the time I wrap up here, I'm going to need to investigate."

I frowned. That was the last thing I wanted.

"We'll find him," I promised.

Even though I didn't have any leads, I would find him —even if it meant making an idiot of myself in the process.

"Good luck with that." One of Parker's colleagues called his name behind him, and he took a step back, his tie flapping over his shoulder as the wind lifted it. "I've got to go. We're still doing dinner this weekend?"

I nodded. "Of course."

I wasn't sure why, but I had to force myself to sound cheerful.

It didn't make sense because Parker was handsome. I mean, he and Brad Pitt had a lot of similarities. I mean *a lot.*

Even though I was dating Parker, my thoughts often went to Riley. The two were complete opposites. Turns out Riley had an ex-fiancée that had still thought she was his current fiancée. I hadn't known about her at all, until I did know about her. Long story short, he'd broken my heart, even though we hadn't known each other long enough for me to officially say that without sounding pathetic. Then he'd followed her back to California.

I had decided to get over him, so I started dating Parker.

Then Riley came back from California. And he was apparently single again.

But I was still dating Parker.

Since I'd given this relationship a shot, I figured I might as well see it through.

So that was what I was doing.

But as I watched Parker walk away, I had to wonder what exactly I was thinking.

———

I sat back in my van and remembered Parker's words about this apartment complex.

Then I locked my doors.

But I didn't bother to move yet.

Instead, I pulled out the handy-dandy notebook from my purse and began to jot a few things down. Writing things down always helped me sort my thoughts out.

Right now, I wanted to make a list of my potential suspects.

To start with, there was Anthony, the friend who'd set up the final arrangements for Earl. Was he hoping to get something from his friend's death? Did he have a stake in Earl's will?

Next, there was Gus, who worked for CIA. He and Earl had made a bucket list together. But how did that fit in with what had happened?

Then there was Sheila, the hospice nurse. I didn't think she had killed him. She didn't look like the type to have a crush on somebody like Earl. Plus, she'd been wearing a wedding ring.

Did home health care workers ever fall in love with their patients?

That seemed like a Lifetime movie in the making. I didn't really want to think about that.

And there was Daphne, the ex-wife. The one who'd said that Earl had discovered a fountain of youth. What had that meant? And what if Earl did have life insurance? Did Daphne have a stake in that?

None of the neighbors knew anything about Earl.

But someone had obviously been keeping an eye on Earl's place. They'd been waiting for the opportunity to come and nab him.

It was like I had talked about with both Toby and Parker. The question was why.

Until I could figure out *why* someone might steal a body, I didn't think I'd find out who had potentially killed him and then taken him.

I supposed it could be two different people.

One killed him. One stole him.

I frowned.

What was I supposed to do with that theory?

There was only one thing I could think to do.

I needed to go back to Earl's house.

I hadn't fully checked things out. Maybe there was some type of clue left behind that would help me find some answers.

CHAPTER 11
3:46 P.M

I STILL HAD the key to Earl's place, and Toby wasn't back yet.

I assumed he and Steve, my male look-alike—an image that still disturbed me—were moving more bodies.

It was still daylight outside, thankfully. Even though the nighttime wasn't inherently more dangerous, somehow it felt that way. Shadows could hide too many things.

And nighttime was when the cockroaches came out.

I cleaned a house once after a double murder. The electricity in the place was out—apparently, the owner hadn't paid the bill in months—and I'd come at night. Anyway, in the process of setting up my own lights inside, I accidentally touched the wall.

It was moving.

That was because cockroaches covered the interior surfaces of the entire house.

I still shivered when I thought about that.

I slipped inside Earl's place and glanced around a moment. Unlike when I was here before, this time I couldn't help but think about how I might be disturbing a crime scene.

But Parker hadn't rushed to come here and check things out.

He was probably waiting until there was something more definite before he did anything.

I paced the living room but didn't see anything that offered any clues.

Next, I went to the kitchen.

My gaze stopped on that card I'd seen earlier.

Get well soon.

It had seemed like such a strange message to send a dying man.

But . . . an idea began to form in my mind.

If Earl had honestly thought he'd found a fountain of youth, then what if this greeting card was appropriate? What if he'd told someone else what he'd discovered and that's why this person had sent him a get well soon card?

I searched the room for a trashcan and found it underneath the kitchen sink. When I pulled the container out, a terrible stench filled the air.

Banana peels, wadded up paper towels, and an old disposable coffee cup waited inside.

I really didn't want to pick through this.

But for the sake of answers, I would. Besides, I'd picked through worse.

I grabbed a clean paper towel so I wouldn't have to touch anything and then began to dig through some of the contents of the trashcan.

Maybe I could find the return envelope in here somewhere and that would give me a clue as to who the sender of the card had been.

I searched through everything, and it wasn't there, nor did I find any other clues.

That was a waste—literally and figuratively.

I put everything back in the trashcan and washed my hands.

Then I stared at the hallway leading to the other end of the house.

There could be some type of evidence there.

The only way to find out would be to search.

———

I didn't find anything in Earl's guestroom or bathroom.

But as I stood in the center of Earl's bedroom and stared at his empty bed, my phone rang.

It was Nurse Sheila. I'd left her my number in case she remembered anything. I hoped she had.

"Ms. St. Claire," she started. "I did remember something, and it might not seem like much. But I wanted to mention it to you, just in case."

"Yes. Of course."

"It's not necessarily about who visited him," she said. "But I thought it might be worth mentioning that, on the day that Earl died, I was there in the morning. He was having a gastrointestinal issue."

"Gastrointestinal?"

"Yes, his stomach hurt."

I wasn't sure how that fit—or if it fit. But I wanted to cover all my bases. "Did you tell the physician who came to declare him dead?"

"I did mention it," Sheila's voice softened. "But, considering Earl's cancer, it wasn't entirely unusual."

"Thanks so much for letting me know." I shoved the phone back into my pocket.

A gastrointestinal issue. I wasn't sure if that would help me find any answers or not. In fact, it was probably as irrelevant as a has-been actor from the nineties.

As I glanced at Earl's bed, something peeking out from the sheets caught my eye, and I stepped closer.

I picked up a small plastic wrapper—the kind that usually went around the tops of bottles of liquid medicine as a safety precaution. I could barely make out the words on it.

I thought it said Ipecac.

Ipecac?

Wasn't that used to make people throw up after they'd ingested poison?

I quickly double-checked that fact on my phone.

I was right. It was.

However, it was no longer recommended that people use the medicine because of side effects. I was surprised you could still buy it, but apparently you could.

Was Earl having stomach issues and taking something to make him throw up?

Was he a drug mule? That still didn't make sense to me since he hadn't traveled outside the country. And I couldn't see how anyone could be a drug mule if they were just staying in the same place.

I sighed and paced over to the trashcan in the corner. A couple pieces of paper rested at the bottom.

The first was an invoice from Just Chill dated six weeks ago.

I took note of the client's name, Linda Poppins,

and phone number—not that I thought they were significant. But it did seem strange that the paper was in Earl's trashcan now when it was such an old invoice. Certainly, the trash had been taken out since then.

Right beneath that invoice was an . . . envelope . . . a mint-green envelope that would fit a greeting card.

My breath caught.

Could this be from the same person who'd sent Earl that get well soon card?

I glanced at the handwriting.

The scribble looked familiar. Small and condensed.

I bet this *was* the envelope I'd been looking for!

My heart rate quickened.

However, there was no return address on it.

Go figure.

The postmark was from Norfolk, and it was dated five days ago.

I held the envelope to the light. I'd read about the old trick in Nancy Drew books growing up, but sometimes it did work.

I squinted. There appeared to be some type of indentation on the paper.

I scrambled to the dresser and found a pencil. Then I ran it across the envelope to see if I could pick up on any hidden words.

My breath caught at what I read there.

It said CIA.

My heart beat harder.

Could Gus be behind Earl's death? But why?

Just because someone sent Earl a get-well card did not mean this person killed him. I had to slow my thoughts and really think this through a bit more. Maybe even talk it over with someone. Someone who was my opposite. Who was grounded and logical and lawyer-like.

Someone like Riley.

I glanced at my watch. He *had* told me that if I needed anything I could call him.

He was a sincere guy so I could only assume he'd meant those words.

Then I glanced at that invoice in my hands again.

Was it significant? Did this HVAC invoice somehow tie in with Earl's death?

There was only one way to find out.

I CLEARED my throat as I waited for Linda Poppins to answer the phone.

She did on the third ring.

I sucked in a breath and turned toward the window as I composed myself. "Hello, this is Gabby, and I'm with Just Chill HVAC Services."

"Yes . . ." Just based on the woman's proper voice, an image of an older, cultured aristocrat filled my mind.

"We performed services at your house about a month and a half ago," I continued.

"I remember."

"I was just following up to see how our technician did. We're hoping he did a super job." A *supercalifragilisticexpialidocious* job.

I stopped myself before saying that. However, just

her last name alone had ignited so many songs inside me.

She paused a moment before saying, "I suppose he did fine. I barely remember he was here even."

"So no problems or complaints?"

"No."

"Was Earl courteous and did he answer all of your questions?"

"He was fine. I didn't have any questions. He was quiet and stayed to himself. I can't complain."

"Wonderful news." I put on my cheeriest, most professional voice. After all, a spoonful of sugar did help the phone surveys go down. "That's all I need to know. Thank you so much for your time."

She suddenly gasped. "Did you hear that?"

I froze. "Hear what?"

"The squirrels," she muttered. "They're back again. Oh, those squirrels! I swear they're going to make me lose my mind!"

With a strangled cry of frustration, the call ended.

Squirrels? What was she talking about?

I stared at my phone and frowned. That hadn't gotten me anywhere.

Maybe Mrs. Poppins wasn't connected to this at all.

Right now, I needed to talk to Gus again.

Thankfully, I'd called Riley so I could bounce some ideas off him, and he'd volunteered to come with me to the CIA.

I picked him up and gave him the latest updates as I drove.

"One thing is for sure. Life is never dull when you're around." He flashed me a smile.

"Thank you." I actually wasn't sure if he meant that as a compliment or not, but I was going to consider it one.

We pulled up at the animal shelter, which closed in under an hour. So I'd gotten here just in the nick of time.

As we climbed from my vehicle, I paused.

There at the back of the building sat a silver sedan.

And I couldn't be sure because of the grainy video, but it appeared to match the one I'd seen in that video.

"What is it?" Riley asked.

I pointed. "That looks like the car. The one Earl's body was in. I need to check it out."

Before Riley could stop me, I rushed toward the vehicle. No one was out here so I should be okay.

But when I peered inside the sedan, it looked

clean. I didn't know what I was expecting to see. A body bag. A signed letter of murderous intent. An ACME bomb.

There was nothing but some old fast-food wrappers and a sweatshirt.

"You know there are a lot of cars on the road that look like this," Riley reminded me as he caught up with me. "Silver sedans are popular."

"I know. But I feel certain that this one's it. Gus must be our guy."

Riley twisted his head, not appearing totally convinced. "Then let's go talk to him and see what he has to say."

CHAPTER 13
4:21 P.M

AS I WALKED into the shelter, I glanced at the doors as I passed.

One was cracked open.

I peered inside and spotted Megan.

I sucked in a breath when I saw her sitting upside down in her chair with a white and brown cream of some sort spread across her face. Her eyes were closed so she didn't see me. "If I Could Turn Back Time" played on a small speaker in the corner.

"Is she okay?" Riley leaned close and gawked at the woman.

"If I had to guess, she's just trying to look younger."

"What?"

"Long story." I motioned for him to keep following me.

I hurried past her office to Gus's. I didn't bother to knock. Instead, I charged inside.

Gus looked up from his desk, surprise washing over his features. "You . . . what are you doing back here?"

Riley slipped inside behind me and shut the door.

"Did you kill Earl?" I blurted.

Gus's eyes became even wider. "What? No. Why would I do that?"

"That's what I'm trying to figure out. Why *would* you do that? What did he do to you?"

"Nothing." He raised his hands in alarm. "He didn't do anything to me. I don't know what you're talking about."

"I know what Earl was hiding. I told you I'm a private investigator. Earl actually hired me before he passed. He felt like he was being watched."

"He did?"

I nodded. "He did. Now I'm trying to wrap up loose ends. Just in case . . ."

He raised an eyebrow as he stared at me skeptically. "And you know what Earl was hiding, you said? The only thing he was hiding was that fantasy he had about getting rich and buying his way to good health."

I kept my expression neutral. "I know all about

his get rich plans. He thought money would be the answer to all his problems."

"Yes, he did. He had all kinds of crazy plans."

"He never told me about those. Like what?"

Gus stared at me.

I shrugged. "He's dead now. Why does it matter?"

"True, I guess. His favorite was that one about stealing a diamond."

Stealing a diamond?

Interesting . . .

I tried to keep my poker face. "Tell me more."

"All I know is Earl—before he went into hospice—did some work at this rich lady's house. She hardly noticed him at all. But as he was working in the bathroom, he heard her voice carry from down the hallway. She was talking to her insurance broker about her jewelry collection. Apparently, she had a diamond that was worth thirty thousand dollars."

"Thirty thousand dollars?" I let out a low whistle. "That's a lot of money."

I remembered that invoice I'd found in the trash—the one for Mrs. Poppins. That had to be the house where he'd been working. That was why he'd saved the invoice!

"Earl thought that was pretty impressive too. He

played around with some ideas about how he might be able to get his hands on it, how it would solve all his problems."

Realization dawned on me. "It could be like the fountain of youth."

Gus snapped his fingers. "Exactly. He kept thinking if he could find some type of windfall, he could buy his way into some better medical treatment."

More facts clicked in my mind. "Is that why you sent him the card that said get well soon?"

Surprise sparked in his gaze. "He was trying to keep the hope alive, and I was trying to keep it alive with him. Just trying to be a good friend."

I crossed my arms as I stared him down, using my intense investigator look. "So you didn't steal this diamond?"

"Steal it? Why would I steal it?" His voice climbed in pitch as he responded.

While he talked, I glanced behind him and spotted a group of animal shelter employees in a picture on his bookshelf. Gus wore a blue polo shirt in the photo, but three of the men wore green shirts.

Gus followed my gaze. "Something caught your eye?"

"Is that Earl in the picture?"

He shrugged. "Yeah, he worked here for about a month when he was between jobs. It didn't pan out. Turns out Earl doesn't like animals. Then he got the new job with Just Chill. Why?"

I stored that fact away. But there was something else about that photo . . . "You're wearing a blue shirt. Why are some of the other guys wearing a different color?"

"Because I'm an administrator, and they're the men on the street."

My mind flashed back to the green I'd seen under Earl's fingernails.

I knew it wasn't carpet fibers, but could it be from . . . one of those polo shirts?

"Was Earl friends with any of those men?" I asked.

"Yeah, of course. Berkley in particular. Why?"

Riley and I exchanged a glance.

"Who's Berkley?" Riley asked. "Tell us about him."

"He's one of our dogcatchers. He's not really a dogcatcher, but he picks up any animals that need a home, so that's what we call him."

Riley and I exchanged another glance.

"Where is Berkley right now?" I asked.

"He took one of our dogs to the vet," Gus said. "A

little chow chow needs to be fixed tomorrow morning, so the vet asked if we could bring him early so they could keep him in a kennel at the clinic overnight."

My heart beat harder. "Do you know what vet?"

"I'm not sure where you're going with this." Gus squirmed before steeling his gaze again.

"I just want to have a talk with Berkley. That's all. I promise."

He let out a long breath. "We have a vet down the road who does a lot of stuff for us for super cheap. Midway Veterinary. That's where Berkley and Chow Mein should be."

Without saying anything else, Riley and I took off toward my van.

We needed to get to the vet.

Now.

———

As soon as I stepped outside, my phone rang.

It was Parker.

I braced myself for whatever he would say, trying to prepare for the possibility that this could turn ugly.

I could be arrested.

Toby could take over my apartment.

Riley would think of me as the freak who could clean up after a crime but couldn't keep track of a dead body.

I might even make a list of "World's Most Stupidest Criminals."

I cleared my throat before saying, "Hello?"

"Gabby, I just wanted to give you an update," he started.

Okay . . . so far, so good. "About what?"

"You mentioned a silver sedan with a foot hanging out the back."

"That's correct."

"I keep getting calls about that foot," he said. "Apparently, it fell off on the interstate."

"What?" I tried not to gag as an image of that filled my mind.

"It fell off because it wasn't a real foot," he added dryly. "It was a mannequin. People on the road didn't know that, though. The driver is some wannabe clothing designer who's trying to pass her finals. She bought the mannequin used from someone who lives in Norfolk."

Wait . . . so the silver sedan was a false lead this whole time? I gave myself a mental scolding.

"Thanks for letting me know," I muttered.

"I'm wrapping up things here, but I plan to head out to talk to you about this missing corpse afterward."

"Of course. I'll text you the address."

If I didn't forget . . .

I ended the call and gave Riley the update.

My mind raced . . .

"What is it?" Riley asked as he shifted beside me.

"The neighbor said his dogs had a barking fit about fifteen minutes before I talked to him—that would be right around the time Earl disappeared. He said they always bark at certain things: the mailman, the doorbell . . ."

"Okay . . ."

"And probably the dogcatcher, right? It makes sense."

"I suppose."

"In that video I saw, there was an animal control vehicle that passed on the screen before the silver sedan."

"Keep going."

"If the killer drove an animal control vehicle, he could've easily slipped the body into the back." I spoke my contemplations aloud, my words coming out nearly as fast as my thoughts swirled. "Maybe in one of the compartments used for the larger dogs."

"But why would he do that?"

An idea had formed in my mind. I wasn't sure if it made any sense, but I hoped it did. "What if Earl and Berkley started talking about these side hustles, and Earl mentioned this woman with this expensive diamond? What if they concocted a plan?"

Riley tilted his head in doubt, his eyes narrowed. "I still don't know what this has to do with Earl's death."

I put my van into Drive and took off down the road. "Parker mentioned that maybe Earl was a drug mule. I knew that didn't make sense. But what if Berkley decided to enact that grand larceny himself? What if he got the diamond somehow and then went to show it to Earl?"

"Would Earl be impressed or upset?" Riley asked.

"Exactly the question! Earl would want some of that payout." My thoughts continued to race. "So what if when Earl realized the windfall his friend was going to receive, he decided in a fit of selfish rage to swallow the diamond so Berkley couldn't keep it."

"That's an interesting theory." His eyes lit with consideration.

"That would explain Earl's digestive issues. Maybe Berkley brought that medicine and made him throw up so he could get that diamond back. But either it didn't work or he was interrupted."

Riley leaned back as if thinking through what I'd said. "Or the medicine may have killed him . . ."

"That's it!" My hand hit the steering wheel—and, by default, the horn.

I flinched at the sound.

Riley ignored it. "Then Berkley had to think of another way to retrieve that diamond. And now this Berkley guy is at the vet because . . ." He frowned and paused as if he couldn't finish that thought.

But I could. "Clearly, he wasn't able to wait for Earl to pass the diamond from his system because Earl died. The only other way Berkley will get the large payout that will come with the diamond is to—"

"Cut it from Earl's stomach." Riley frowned as if the idea appalled him. "That's quite some theory."

"It is. But I think it may have some validity."

"I think you might be right," Riley admitted with another frown.

We pulled to a stop in front of the veterinary office.

Sure enough, a truck from CIA was parked in the back.

But no other cars were in the lot.

In fact, the office appeared to already be closed. Maybe Berkley had a key because he came here so often to take animals in for their care.

Riley and I exchanged another look.

If Berkley was inside, and if he did have Earl's body, then things could turn really ugly.

We needed to figure out exactly how we were going to proceed.

CHAPTER 14
4:51 P.M

"WE DON'T HAVE ANY PROOF," I told Riley as I stared at the vet's office.

The place was painted bright pink and sat off a side street in Norfolk. That worked to our advantage right now since no one would most likely see us.

"We could call the police right now, but we're just going off a theory," I muttered.

"True." Riley crossed his arms and stared at the building also. "But if we go in there and confront Berkley, we could be putting ourselves in danger."

I nibbled on my lip. I had to do something! "I need to at least peek inside. I need to see what he's doing. If I see Earl's body, we'll call the police. If I don't, we'll leave. Sound like a plan?"

Riley gave me a look. "I guess that sounds reasonable enough."

I released my breath. Good. We'd come to an agreement.

I opened the car door and stepped out. Carefully, I made my way around to the side of the building. I needed to find a window.

While I did that, Riley paced toward the dog catcher truck. Riley tried to open a couple of the compartments, but they were locked.

I found a couple of windows, but they both had closed blinds I couldn't see through.

This was going to be more difficult than I'd hoped.

"Gabby, look at this," Riley called.

I hurried toward him. He pointed to a string caught on one of the hinges.

"What color pajamas was Earl wearing when you were supposed to pick him up?"

"Pale yellow." Realization washed over me. This string was also yellow. "This could be the clue we're looking for."

"Could you see inside the windows?" Riley studied my face as he waited for my answer.

"The shades are all closed."

Riley frowned and rubbed his jaw. "These fibers on the hinges aren't going to be enough to prove anything."

"I just need a better look." I stared at the building

with a frown.

"How do you propose you get that better look?"

"I need to get inside."

"Gabby . . ." Warning marred his voice.

"Maybe Berkley left a door unlocked. I'll be careful. Why don't you wait out here? If I don't come out soon, call the police." I didn't want to put Riley's law career at risk by giving him a criminal record.

"There's no way I'm letting you go in there alone." He crossed his arms and shook his head.

"I'm going in," I muttered.

He frowned. "Then I'll be right behind you."

With a sigh, I tugged on the back door.

It wasn't latched.

Sure, the place was closed. But if the door wasn't locked . . . it was practically an invitation to come inside. How was I to know?

I slowly opened the door and stepped inside.

The hallway was clear.

I motioned for Riley to follow.

I crept farther in, listening for telltale noises with every step. It was hard to hear over a dog barking in a nearby kennel.

Was that Chow Mein?

I glanced through a glass divider into the kennel area and spotted the dog. He stared at us, a curious look in his eyes. Thankfully, he'd been barking before we'd stepped inside.

Someone was in the examination room two doors down.

Someone who was whistling.

What song was that? I couldn't place it right now. But I knew it was going to bug me until I figured it out.

I didn't hear any other dogs.

I've got an abysmal feeling . . .

The song played over and over in my head.

I reached the doorway and slowly peered around it.

I sucked in a breath when I saw Berkley inside . . . and Earl laid out on the exam table in front of him.

Berkley had a scalpel raised above him as he continued to whistle. That's when I recognized the tune.

"Diamonds Are a Girl's Best Friend."

————

Before I could figure out what to do, a noise cut through the air.

"Hicktown" by Jason Aldean.

I'd programmed that ringtone just for . . . Toby.

I swallowed hard before grabbing my phone and silencing it.

But I was too late.

Berkley swirled toward me, scalpel still in hand.

I recognized him immediately. He was the chicken guy who'd said he owed me one . . .

"Who are you?" he demanded, his gaze skittering between me and Riley.

I narrowed my gaze at him. "You stole my dead body."

"I . . . what?" He squinted.

"I need to get Earl's body to the funeral home before Toby loses his job, moves in with me, and makes me lose my mind by incessantly talking about toe jam."

"What?" Riley muttered behind me.

"Long story."

"You don't understand." Berkley held out the scalpel, his arm shaking. "Earl has something that's mine, and I need to get it. I was going to return his body. I don't care what happens to Earl."

"Of course not. You just care about the thirty thousand-dollar diamond that he swallowed."

Sweat poured down his face. "How did you know?"

"Because I've been trying to track him all day. That's how. What I'm not sure about is how you got the diamond." I thought I could still make a run for it if it came down to it, so I figured it wouldn't hurt to ask for some details here. If not, at least I'd die with answers.

"He told me about the diamond at that lady's house, and I knew it was an answer to prayer."

"Okay . . . but how did you get the diamond?" I tried to put a better picture together in my head.

"I knew I needed an excuse to get inside that house. It had been several weeks since Earl did his HVAC job there, so I wasn't even sure where this diamond was. So I got creative. I released a squirrel into her house. I figured she'd call CIA—we're number one on the search engine for wildlife removal."

"That's thinking outside the box," I muttered. "And that explains Mrs. Poppins's squirrel paranoia."

"It worked! That woman refused to go back inside the house—she was panicked—and when I got there, I had the whole place to myself. I grabbed the diamond, replaced it with a fake one, found the squirrel, and got out of there."

"Then you took it to show Earl? The diamond," I clarified. "Not the squirrel."

"I did."

"But why would you do that?" It seemed risky and unnecessary.

"We became fast friends when he worked for the shelter. I figured he was dying soon, that he wouldn't care. But he did." Berkley's scowl deepened. "He said the diamond was rightfully his because he was going to steal it first and that the money from something like that could afford him better medical treatment. He was just waiting for some time to pass before going back to take it, so he wouldn't automatically be a suspect."

"But you got to it first. So you showed it to him, and he swallowed it?"

Berkley scowled. "Earl was impulsive like that. But I still couldn't believe he did it."

"What happened then?" Riley asked.

"I tried to get him to gag it out, but he wouldn't. Then the nurse pulled into the driveway. I panicked. I had to run."

"You ran out the back door, didn't you?"

"I always used the back door. No one would see me that way."

A timeline began to form in my mind. "Because you clearly went back at some point."

"I waited until later. In the meantime, I went to the store and got some medicine to make him throw up. I went back that night and forced him to swallow the liquid."

"And?"

Berkley shook his head, sweat covering his skin. "And . . . I don't know what happened. But Earl started having a seizure or something. I didn't mean to kill him!"

"There's this thing called mixing medicines." I didn't mean to sound condescending, but maybe I did. Still . . . "You shouldn't do it. Some of them create terrible reactions."

The sweat now began to trickle down his face. "I didn't think about that. I just wanted the diamond. Anyway, I panicked and ran, but I knew I had to go back again. I couldn't let Earl be buried with that diamond in his belly. That gemstone could change my life."

"Makes sense. Why did you wait so long to go back?"

"I didn't know what to do. I started to go more than once and then changed my mind. Then I saw you guys show up. I knew I didn't have much time. As soon as I saw you in the backyard, I knew I had to make my move."

I nodded at Earl. "And now you're going to cut into his body to retrieve it. You think it's in the stomach or the intestines by now?"

"How should I know?" He stared at me like I was the crazy one holding a scalpel over a dead body. "Do I look like a doctor or something?"

"Dr. Jekyll/Mr. Hyde maybe."

"You shouldn't have come here." He lunged at me with his scalpel.

Before the blade hit me, Riley jerked me back and pushed himself in front of me.

My heart pounded as I stared at Berkley and that crazy look in his eyes.

What was going to happen now?

What if I got Riley killed?

"You don't want to do that," Riley warned, his body crouched and ready to act.

"I just need this diamond!" Berkley's voice cracked. "You two weren't supposed to be here!"

"I have to get that body to the funeral home," I told him. "You don't even understand what's at stake here."

"What?" Berkley wrinkled his brow with confusion.

Before anyone could say anything else, the back door slammed open, and Parker and several officers flooded inside and rushed toward Berkley.

"Freeze! Hands up! Don't move."

Three seconds later, they'd taken his scalpel and handcuffed him.

"Parker?" I muttered as I stared at him in confusion. "How did you know?"

"I texted him," Riley admitted.

Realization washed over me. "I suppose that was only wise."

"The only thing that would have been wiser would have been if you texted me instead." Parker gave me a look as he paused beside us.

"I would have . . . eventually."

Parker's gaze flickered from me to Riley then back to me again. Finally, he squeezed my arm, "Good job, Nancy Drew."

A small sense of satisfaction washed through me. "Thanks."

"But next time, text me yourself."

CHAPTER 15
5:56 P.M

AN HOUR LATER, Earl Mansfield had been picked up by the medical examiner. He would have a full autopsy to look into his death, even though Riley and I had heard Berkley's confession ourselves.

Berkley had forced Earl to take that medicine in order to puke up the diamond, and it had ultimately killed the man.

Berkley would most likely be going away for a long time—for involuntary manslaughter, obstruction of justice, and grand larceny.

Meanwhile, hopefully Mrs. Poppins would get her diamond back. Maybe she could even go fly a kite to celebrate.

Toby had called his boss and told the man his own version of what had happened today. Somehow,

Toby and his half-witted antics had ended up being praised as a hero, and I'd even heard something about a promotion.

Riley had been by my side through all of it, listening and supporting me.

"Everything has a way of working out, doesn't it?" Riley turned toward me as we lingered in the waiting room at Midway Veterinary.

"It does."

He glanced back at the chow who still barked at us from the kennel. "Can you ever see yourself having a dog?"

"Not really."

"But if you did . . . what would you name it?"

I thought about it a moment. "Oh, I don't know. Maybe . . . Watson."

"Watson? Not Sherlock?"

"I'm Sherlock, of course."

He chuckled. "I like the way you think."

"I'm glad you like the way I think." I tried to hide my grin—especially as Parker reappeared around the corner.

I was pretty sure he was finished questioning us, and we could leave, but I didn't want to go yet. I wanted to see everything get wrapped up.

And it appeared that's what was happening.

At just that moment, Sierra stepped inside also, holding something in her hands.

A cat.

"I heard you guys were here," she started.

"Who told you?"

"I went to the CIA, and Gus mentioned it." She held up the tabby in her arms. "Look at my newest family member."

"You got another cat?" I stroked the kitty's head.

"I couldn't walk away from the shelter after hearing about that hoarding situation and not bring one of these beauties home with me."

I didn't mention to Sierra that she might have a cat hoarding situation on her hands at some point also. But she looked happy, so I was happy for her . . . *and* I didn't feel as guilty for not adopting a cat myself.

"Did you name him or her?" I asked.

"I was thinking about Earl," she muttered. "What do you think?"

I moaned. "No, definitely not. But I won't tell our landlord that you've well surpassed our two-pet limit."

We all laughed.

I was so glad these people were in my life.

Because who else would put up with my shenanigans?

~~~

Thank you for reading *Half Witted*. If you enjoyed this book, please consider leaving a review.

Stay tuned for *Half Truth*, coming soon!

~~~

ALSO BY CHRISTY BARRITT:

YOU MIGHT ALSO ENJOY

. . .

THE SQUEAKY CLEAN MYSTERY
SERIES

On her way to completing a degree in forensic science, Gabby St. Claire drops out of school and starts her own crime-scene cleaning business. When a routine cleaning job uncovers a murder weapon the police overlooked, she realizes that the wrong person is in jail. She also realizes that crime scene cleaning might be the perfect career for utilizing her investigative skills.

#1 Hazardous Duty

#2 Suspicious Minds

#2.5 It Came Upon a Midnight Crime (novella)

#3 Organized Grime

#4 Dirty Deeds

#5 The Scum of All Fears

#6 To Love, Honor and Perish

HOLLY ANNA PALADIN MYSTERIES

When Holly Anna Paladin is given a year to live, she embraces her final days doing what she loves most—random acts of kindness. But when one of her extreme good deeds goes horribly wrong, implicating Holly in a string of murders, Holly is suddenly in a different kind of fight for her life. She knows one thing for sure: she only has a short amount of time to make a difference. And if helping the people she cares about puts her in danger, it's a risk worth taking.

THE WORST DETECTIVE EVER

I'm not really a private detective. I just play one on TV.

Joey Darling, better known to the world as Raven Remington, detective extraordinaire, is trying to separate herself from her invincible alter ego. She played the spunky character for five years on the hit TV show *Relentless*, which catapulted her to fame and into the role of Hollywood's sweetheart. When her marriage falls apart, her finances dwindle to nothing, and her father disappears, Joey finds herself on the Outer Banks of North Carolina, trying to piece together her life away from the limelight. But as people continually mistake her for the character she played on TV, she's tasked with solving real life crimes . . . even though she's terrible at it.

COMPLETE BOOK LIST

Squeaky Clean Mysteries:
  #1 Hazardous Duty
  #2 Suspicious Minds
  #2.5 It Came Upon a Midnight Crime (novella)
  #3 Organized Grime
  #4 Dirty Deeds
  #5 The Scum of All Fears
  #6 To Love, Honor and Perish
  #7 Mucky Streak
  #8 Foul Play
  #9 Broom & Gloom
  #10 Dust and Obey
  #11 Thrill Squeaker
  #11.5 Swept Away (novella)
  #12 Cunning Attractions
  #13 Cold Case: Clean Getaway

#14 Cold Case: Clean Sweep

#15 Cold Case: Clean Break

#16 Cleans to an End

While You Were Sweeping, A Riley Thomas Spinoff

The Sierra Files:

#1 Pounced

#2 Hunted

#3 Pranced

#4 Rattled

The Gabby St. Claire Diaries (a Tween Mystery series):

#1 The Curtain Call Caper

#2 The Disappearing Dog Dilemma

#3 The Bungled Bike Burglaries

The Worst Detective Ever

#1 Ready to Fumble

#2 Reign of Error

#3 Safety in Blunders

#4 Join the Flub

#5 Blooper Freak

#6 Flaw Abiding Citizen

#7 Gaffe Out Loud

#8 Joke and Dagger

#9 Wreck the Halls

#10 Glitch and Famous

#11 Not on My Botch

Raven Remington

Relentless

Holly Anna Paladin Mysteries:

#1 Random Acts of Murder

#2 Random Acts of Deceit

#2.5 Random Acts of Scrooge

#3 Random Acts of Malice

#4 Random Acts of Greed

#5 Random Acts of Fraud

#6 Random Acts of Outrage

#7 Random Acts of Iniquity

Lantern Beach Mysteries

#1 Hidden Currents

#2 Flood Watch

#3 Storm Surge

#4 Dangerous Waters

#5 Perilous Riptide

#6 Deadly Undertow

Lantern Beach Romantic Suspense

#1 Tides of Deception

#2 Shadow of Intrigue

#3 Storm of Doubt

#4 Winds of Danger

#5 Rains of Remorse

#6 Torrents of Fear

Lantern Beach P.D.

#1 On the Lookout

#2 Attempt to Locate

#3 First Degree Murder

#4 Dead on Arrival

#5 Plan of Action

Lantern Beach Escape

Afterglow (a novelette)

Lantern Beach Blackout

#1 Dark Water

#2 Safe Harbor

#3 Ripple Effect

#4 Rising Tide

Lantern Beach Guardians

#1 Hide and Seek

#2 Shock and Awe

#3 Safe and Sound

Lantern Beach Blackout: The New Recruits

#1 Rocco

#2 Axel

#3 Beckett

#4 Gabe

Lantern Beach Mayday

#1 Run Aground

#2 Dead Reckoning

#3 Tipping Point

Lantern Beach Blackout: Danger Rising

#1 Brandon

#2 Dylan

#3 Maddox

#4 Titus

Lantern Beach Christmas

Silent Night

Crime á la Mode

#1 Dead Man's Float

#2 Milkshake Up

#3 Bomb Pop Threat

#4 Banana Split Personalities

Beach Bound Books and Beans Mysteries

#1 Bound by Murder

#2 Bound by Disaster

#3 Bound by Mystery

#4 Bound by Trouble

#5 Bound by Mayhem

Vanishing Ranch

#1 Forgotten Secrets

#2 Necessary Risk

#3 Risky Ambition

#4 Deadly Intent

#5 Lethal Betrayal

#6 High Stakes Deception

#7 Fatal Vendetta

#8 Troubled Tidings

#9 Narrow Escape

The Sidekick's Survival Guide

#1 The Art of Eavesdropping

#2 The Perks of Meddling

#3 The Exercise of Interfering

#4 The Practice of Prying

#5 The Skill of Snooping

#6 The Craft of Being Covert

Saltwater Cowboys

#1 Saltwater Cowboy

#2 Breakwater Protector

#3 Cape Corral Keeper

#4 Seagrass Secrets

#5 Driftwood Danger

#6 Unwavering Security

Beach House Mysteries

#1 The Cottage on Ghost Lane

#2 The Inn on Hanging Hill

#3 The House on Dagger Point

School of Hard Rocks Mysteries

#1 The Treble with Murder

#2 Crime Strikes a Chord

#3 Tone Death

Carolina Moon Series

#1 Home Before Dark

#2 Gone By Dark

#3 Wait Until Dark

#4 Light the Dark

#5 Taken By Dark

Suburban Sleuth Mysteries:

Death of the Couch Potato's Wife

Fog Lake Suspense:

#1 Edge of Peril

#2 Margin of Error

#3 Brink of Danger

#4 Line of Duty

#5 Legacy of Lies

#6 Secrets of Shame

#7 Refuge of Redemption

Cape Thomas Series:

#1 Dubiosity

#2 Disillusioned

#3 Distorted

Standalone Romantic Mystery:

The Good Girl

Suspense:

Imperfect

The Wrecking

Sweet Christmas Novella:

Home to Chestnut Grove

Standalone Romantic-Suspense:

Keeping Guard

The Last Target

Race Against Time

Ricochet

Key Witness

Lifeline

High-Stakes Holiday Reunion

Desperate Measures

Hidden Agenda

Mountain Hideaway

Dark Harbor

Shadow of Suspicion

The Baby Assignment

The Cradle Conspiracy

Trained to Defend

Mountain Survival

Dangerous Mountain Rescue

Nonfiction:

Characters in the Kitchen

Changed: True Stories of Finding God through Christian Music (out of print)

The Novel in Me: The Beginner's Guide to Writing and Publishing a Novel (out of print)

ABOUT THE AUTHOR

USA Today has called Christy Barritt's books "scary, funny, passionate, and quirky."

Christy writes both mystery and romantic suspense novels that are clean with underlying messages of faith. Her books have sold more than three million copies and have won the Daphne du Maurier Award for Excellence in Suspense and Mystery, have been twice nominated for the Romantic Times Reviewers' Choice Award, and have finaled for both a Carol Award and Foreword Magazine's Book of the Year.

She is married to her Prince Charming, a man who thinks she's hilarious—but only when she's not trying to be. Christy is a self-proclaimed klutz, an avid music lover who's known for spontaneously bursting into song, and a road trip aficionado.

When she's not working or spending time with her family, she enjoys singing, playing the guitar, and exploring small, unsuspecting towns where people have no idea how accident-prone she is.

Find Christy online at:
www.christybarritt.com
www.facebook.com/christybarritt
www.twitter.com/cbarritt

Sign up for Christy's newsletter to get information on all of her latest releases here: **www.christybarritt.com/newsletter-sign-up/**

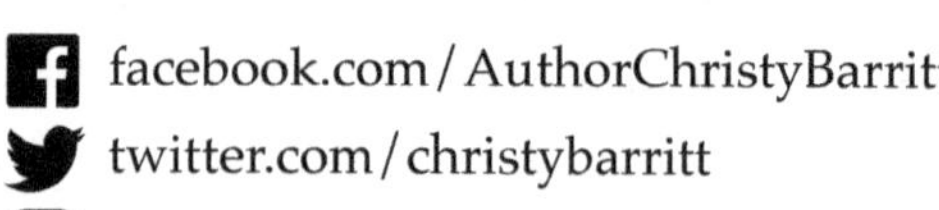

facebook.com / AuthorChristyBarritt
twitter.com / christybarritt
instagram.com / cebarritt